The Rawhider

Center Point
Large Print

Also by Charles N. Heckelmann and available
from Center Point Large Print:

Hell in His Holsters

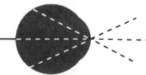

**This Large Print Book carries the
Seal of Approval of N.A.V.H.**

The Rawhider

Charles N. Heckelmann

CENTER POINT LARGE PRINT
THORNDIKE, MAINE

This Center Point Large Print edition is published
in the year 2013 by arrangement with
Golden West Literary Agency.

The characters in this book are entirely imaginary
and have no relation to any living person.

The text of this Large Print edition is unabridged.
In other aspects, this book may
vary from the original edition.
Printed in the United States of America
on permanent paper.
Set in 16-point Times New Roman type.

ISBN: 978-1-61173-813-1

Library of Congress Cataloging-in-Publication Data

Heckelmann, Charles N. (Charles Newman), 1913–2005.
The rawhider / Charles N. Heckelmann.
pages ; cm.
ISBN 978-1-61173-813-1 (library binding : alk. paper)
1. Large type books. I. Title.
PS3515.E1857R39 2013
813′.54—dc23
2013006594

To KAY and BILL

Chapter 1

It was April, 1862, and the North and South were girding themselves for another grim year of fighting.

Success had continued to favour the Confederacy as Price and McCulloch turned back Lyon at Wilson Creek and Grant was whipped at Belmont, Missouri.

Then slowly and inexorably, the picture began to change. In February little Fort Henry on the east bank of the Tennessee River had fallen into Union hands as Lloyd Tilghman's garrison was overwhelmed by two divisions of Grant's infantry attacking overland and a flotilla of gunboats under Foote sweeping upriver.

Finally, Fort Donelson, on the west bank of the Cumberland River, was captured by Grant; and Joe Johnston, with only a few divisions of Confederate troops under his command and no hope for immediate reinforcements, was compelled to abandon the defence of Nashville, thus opening all of Middle Tennessee to the North.

And now, seven weeks later, Grant was methodically gathering men and supplies in preparation for an all-out assault against Corinth,

Mississippi, where Albert Sidney Johnston had collected forty thousand rebel soldiers.

Because the issue at stake was so great—the possession and control of the Mississippi River—Grant had decided not to strike until Buell's Army of the Ohio had marched up from Middle Tennessee to join him. With Buell's help he was sure of taking Corinth. And so he waited, planting a powerful infantry force along the wooded plateau that stretched backward from the Tennessee River at Pittsburg Landing to Shiloh Church, while holding his reserves at Savannah, seven miles away.

For days the flotilla of eighty-two steamboats that had come up from St. Louis to supply Grant's army had plied back and forth between Savannah and Pittsburg Landing, transporting troops and ammunition to the Union lines.

And while Grant waited for Buell, Johnston suddenly decided to take the offensive. Unknown to Sherman and his co-commanders of the five Union divisions at Shiloh, Johnston's army left Corinth on Thursday morning, April 3, marched all that day and the next, and finally bivouacked within a few miles of Sherman's position late Saturday afternoon.

There was no alarm that night. Union sentries patrolled the woods unaware that soldiers in butternut grey were camped almost within shooting range of them. Northern supply packets steamed up and down the river all day Saturday and work on the landing went on without interruption.

Sunday dawned bright and clear. One of the first boats to get up steam was the *Western Star*, a sturdy weather-beaten craft, one hundred and sixty feet long, beam twenty-four feet, and with a spacious hold. It was a shallow-draft steamer from the upper Missouri trade with two big smokestacks and six boilers. The freight deck swarmed with roustabouts. Up and down the gang-plank they toiled, lugging cord wood, bales of grain, sacks of flour, sugar, and tobacco, barrels of molasses, and cases of medical supplies on to the packet.

Bill Horn, the steamboat's owner and pilot, emerged from his cabin high on the texas deck and fastened his moody glance upon the churning surface of the river, half-hidden under a grey dawn mist.

He was a tall man, solidly built in the chest and shoulders, with powerful arms and hands. His hair was coal black and he wore it long in the fashion of the day. A handsome man, not yet thirty, he carried the rigours of sun and wind upon his bronzed, hard-boned face.

Switching his attention from the river, he leaned against the railing, the better to watch the hurried loading operations going on below.

Beyond the landing and a short distance up the

hill was the Cherry Mansion where General Grant had his headquarters. Except for the armed sentries pacing their beats, there was no sign of life around the house. Farther away, across the broad plateau, were the neat windrows of tents marking several infantry regiments. Somewhere in the midst of the camp a bugle sent up its clarion notes and the blue-clad forms of sleepy-eyed soldiers shuffled out of the tents.

As the trumpet notes faded into silence Horn descended to the freight deck. He strode down the landing stage. River packets of all sizes lined the shore. Many of them had steam up in their boilers, ready for a trip to Pittsburg Landing.

Hands thrust deep in his pockets, Horn made his way around the clutter of crates and barrels on the landing. Now and then a roustabout sang out a greeting to him and he answered with a wave of his hand.

He had gone past three moored packets when he caught sight of a newly painted sternwheeler that had arrived late the previous afternoon. It was a sleek-looking craft, its brass work gleaming and a bright new flag whipping from the jack staff.

Horn started to pass the boat when he noticed the name, *The Queen*, painted in huge blue letters on the plank sides of the pilothouse. A startled change came over him. His cheeks stiffened, his long lips grew white and thin, and he swung away from the river.

But he was too late. A tall, stately-looking girl had emerged from the packet and now she walked toward Horn. He stopped and removed his pilot's cap.

The girl gave him an odd, twisting smile and said in a husky voice, "Hello, Bill."

Horn's face didn't change. His mouth maintained its rigid pressure. "Hello, Kay," he murmured.

He looked long and hard at Kay Graham, noting, as he had always noted, the proud way she carried herself, the straight line of her shoulders, the tilt of her well-shaped head, her ash-blond hair and noting, most of all, her eyes which were a deep startling blue.

Seeing her never failed to shock Horn. It was so now—the rich beauty of her, the pull of her personality, the bold strike of her eyes getting deep inside him and upsetting his emotions. He resented her power to stir him, fought against it, and deliberately called upon the memory of things that lay between them to colour the panel of the thoughts with the dark brush of bitterness.

"Aren't you glad to see me?" Kay asked, an elusive teasing note in her voice.

"Should I be?" he responded bluntly.

"You never forget."

He shrugged and said nothing. There was softness in her eyes and warmth, too. She waited for his smile, but it did not come. A hot, angry look flashed in her eyes, then instantly vanished.

"You can be very hard, Bill," she said.

"Sure. As hard as you— when I have to be."

"You still blame me for wrecking the *Missouri Princess*?"

"What do you think? Jed Adams was working for Jack Wade and Wade was working for you. Very simple."

The blue of Kay's eyes deepened in anger. She took a step forward, then stopped.

"You don't believe that, Bill," she said in a low, warning tone. "Wade was on his own when he gave that bribe to Adams."

"Do you remember what you said before we left Fort Benton?" Horn spoke with a hot vehemence. "You were going to beat me to St. Louis and you were going to wind up with a good portion of my business. I'll say this much. You make sure you get what you're going after."

Kay's lips pulled tightly against her even white teeth. She could be as hard as a man when she wanted to be, and she was hard now.

"I've got a reputation for that," she said sharply. "But some day you ought to take the time to ask around about me. I go after things but I go after them straight." She drew herself up straight now and her shoulders seemed to take on width. "I'll match my skill as a pilot with you or any other man on the river. And I can run a business a damned sight better than most. When I go out to beat anyone I do it out in the open where every move I make can be seen. Remember that."

The heat of her talk surprised Horn. He knew Kay Graham as a cool, thoroughly poised woman, equally at ease in the genteel company of women or in the rough and ready company of men. She had a strong will and the boldness to use it to gain what she wanted.

Many a riverman had fallen in love with this beautiful and tempestuous woman. She was known the length and breadth of the Mississippi and was now establishing herself on the Big Muddy. She was the cynosure of all eyes wherever she went. Yet she had given her heart to no man.

She could be warm and friendly when it pleased her. And she could be cold and aloof—almost brutal, at times in the way she shunted aside men who sought to win some meagre token of affection from her.

Now because the memory of anger had turned Horn hostile and indifferent he knew that he had struck a severe blow at her pride. Her emotions were too deeply rooted to tolerate his apathy, his refusal to add further comment. He saw the subtle change in her eyes and realized she was not yet through with him.

"Bill," she said very softly, "you're not fooling me. It isn't the loss of your packet that bothers you. It's Irene. You can't forget her."

Horn's eyes showed the sudden release of temper.

"Leave Irene out of it."

Kay smiled triumphantly.

"You've given her up, but you can't forget her," she said, and then the smile slowly left her face. "She drained you dry, Bill. She took the best that was in you and left a broken shell. She destroyed your faith, your trust in people. No woman is worth that."

He gave her a long, steady look, his deep-socketed eyes very dark and grave.

"I'm thoroughly aware of that," he said harshly.

Suddenly the events of the past year came flooding back upon him in a cold, smothering tide. They, in turn, seemed to reach out farther and farther into the dim recesses of recollection, dredging up other things that could not and would not be forgotten.

He thought of himself as a boy back in St. Louis and of Jack Wade who had grown up in the same frontier town. Somehow they had never got along together. Even as boys a strong undercurrent of hostility had whirled between them.

Horn could not explain it. He could remember their fights, their fierce rivalries which, some-how, had always gone deeper than ordinary youthful rivalries.

Perhaps the reason lay in the fact that Horn had been the son of a prosperous steamboat owner and Wade the son of a poor sawmill worker. Wade had always been envious of Horn. He had never outgrown it.

When Horn had taken over his father's steamboat line Wade, then working as a mere deckhand on a Missouri River packet, had been resentful. Later, Wade had landed a post as pilot with another line backed by a St. Louis gambling syndicate. They had tried to put Horn out of business by slashing their freight and passenger rates and speeding up their runs.

But the Missouri—a capricious, unpredictable river that often changed channels and shifted sand bars overnight—had proved Wade's undoing. Twice in one year Wade had wrecked packets when he grew careless, misjudged the depth of a channel, and crashed into sawyers, ripping the bottoms out of both craft.

Those accidents with their total loss of freight as well as the steamboats themselves (fortunately the passengers had been rescued, on each occasion, by another passing packet) had spelled ruin for the gambling syndicate.

And Wade had been without a job for almost a year after that. Steamboat owners had been reluctant to hire him as a pilot after his unhappy record with the syndicate.

It was not until Kay Graham, one of the best-known pilots on the Upper Mississippi had entered the Missouri River trade that Wade got his second chance. The beautiful young steamboat owner had a reputation for being a shrewd operator, a skilful pilot, and a good judge of men. But somehow she had been taken in by Wade.

He was a handsome devil, tall, fair-skinned, and with light hair that was almost the colour of straw. There was a sleek, well-groomed look about him. He had energy and drive and he did everything with a dash. It was this flair for colour, for conscious gallantry in the presence of women that won their attention, their admiration.

She had been one week on the Missouri when word circulated about St. Louis, Yankton, Omaha, Sioux City, and the river ports that Jack Wade had been hired by Kay Graham as a pilot. And it was at this same time that Wade discovered Irene Nostrum, to whom Horn was engaged, and made his play for her.

Wade, a glib talker, ardent and intense in his expressions of devotion, had won Irene with little trouble. And Horn, busily readying his packets for an early spring trip to Fort Benton in Montana, had been one of the last people to realize what was going on.

He was a man in whom feeling ran deep and true. Finding Irene and loving her had brought a rich fulfilment to his life. She was everything a man could ever hope for. She had fired his ambition to build his steamboat line into one of the best on the Big Muddy.

No suspicion had entered his mind when Irene

began breaking dates on short notice. Even the growing coolness of her manner had not alarmed him, for his own manner was too reserved for him to find significance in the emotional restraint of another.

Then had come the rumours, at first faint and elusive, then gradually more insistent. On two occasions Horn had seen Irene and Wade together. He had said nothing to Irene about it. The break had come when Irene sent a message to the *Western Star*, cancelling an appointment for dinner with Horn because she was ill. That same night Horn had gone to the Palmer House for dinner with several other river pilots. Among the diners that evening he had seen Irene and Jack Wade.

The other pilots noticed Irene at the same moment that Horn did. Before they could say anything Horn had arisen. He looked once at Irene's table. She glanced up, saw him, and her face reddened under his cold-eyed scrutiny. Then he had strode out of the dining room, brushing aside two waiters, and had gone to the nearest saloon and got drunk.

It was the only night rivermen in St. Louis had ever seen Bill Horn with more whisky than he could hold. He left the next morning on the *Western Star*, for Fort Benton and he never knew till later that Irene had tried to see him before he steamed away.

He had never spoken to Irene again. And the crew of the *Western Star* remembered that northern trip because Horn worked them harder than he had ever worked them before. Yet no man among them complained, for he toiled harder than any of them. He drove himself without mercy, trying to forget the gnawing ache in his heart, trying to blot out the black bitterness that filled his mind.

Toward Wade he felt the same continuing contempt. The man was an adventurer. There was no depth to him. He was incapable of a clean, honest emotion. But he blamed Irene for not seeing through the bland, smiling mask to the real man that was Wade underneath.

He made no move against Wade. Not even when the rumour began to spread in Fort Benton (where they had both tied up after a freight and passenger run from St. Louis) that Wade had stolen his girl without a fight. He had deemed it wiser to ignore the issue.

But Wade, relishing his first victory over Horn, had given him no peace. He had crowded Horn into accepting a $5,000 wager to race him from Fort Benton to St. Louis. The offer had been made in a crowded saloon in the presence of rivermen, trappers, fur traders, and miners.

One look at the rough, bearded men at the bar told Horn what they were already thinking of him—that he had backed down once in front of

Wade. They could not understand a man who would not fight for his woman. It did not matter to them that Irene had made her own choice—that she had destroyed the faith in Bill Horn.

If he refused this challenge he was finished on the Big Muddy. Horn knew it. And Wade knew it. So Horn accepted, not realizing he was buying trouble when he hired Jed Adams as co-pilot before leaving Fort Benton.

The race had been close and hard-fought all the way to Yankton. And then, steaming down a wide channel near Sioux City, the *Western Star* had met disaster. Horn had left the pilothouse for a few moments. Jed Adams, with an easy portion of the river to navigate, sent the packet hurtling into a huge sawyer that tore it apart.

A sudden swerve in direction had sent Horn clambering up to the pilothouse from the texas. He had seen the clear stretch of channel ahead. He had seen Adams spin the wheel about, sending the *Western Star* careening toward the near shore.

Horn had moved fast—but not fast enough. He saw the huge trunk of the tree, its roots or branches locked somewhere below in the river mud. Then came the jolting crash as Horn reached the wheel and grappled with Adams.

The *Western Star* had gone to the bottom in ten minutes. Only the presence of a passing upriver packet, which turned to pick up all the survivors, kept the disaster from being more serious.

Horn, with part of his crew, had swum ashore.

And it was there on the river bank that Horn had nearly killed Adams with his bare hands. Dave London and two deck hands finally pulled Horn away. But not before Adams had admitted accepting $500 from Jack Wade to wreck the *Western Star.*

Back in St. Louis Horn had hunted up Wade. They'd fought—bitterly and viciously as only two deeply hating men can fight—but Kay Graham had appeared to break it up.

Horn had made his accusations, then, against Kay. She had denied them strenuously, had refused the $5,000 he stubbornly offered her for the race.

Wade had cleared out of St. Louis. And Irene Nostrum, now fully aware of what she had lost in Bill Horn, had attempted to renew the old affair. He had turned her down, refusing even to speak to her.

He had spent the remainder of the season and most of his capital in raising the *Western Star* and refitting her for service. The war had come then and he'd volunteered for Union service. He'd been rejected because the Northern generals were of the opinion his specialized talents would be wasted in the infantry, and they hinted that they had another job in mind for him—a job suited to his own particular experience.

The only word that had been received about

Wade was that he had joined the Confederates. Where Wade was fighting and in what division Horn had not been able to learn.

Looking again at Kay Graham, Horn found these past events crowding into his mind with a disconcerting sense of reality.

She spoke sharply now and with a tinge of impatience.

"Bill, I'm afraid you misunderstood me when I said no woman was worth the loss of a man's faith. I mean there is too much fun in living and loving to let one woman put a period to your life."

He answered her placidly. "Thanks for the lecture. I've got the *Western Star* and my work to do on the river—a job that needs doing with other men. I reckon that's enough for me."

"Are you altogether sure of that?" she asked.

Before Horn could answer a dull rumble of thunder filled the sky on the far side of the Tennessee. It was a dull, muted roar of sound, swelling in volume, then receding.

Kay threw a startled glance at the sky, at the widening band of grey light far down on the eastern horizon. Then she turned back to Horn.

"Artillery?" she inquired.

"Yeah," he said. "Looks like the fight has started. Johnston must have got tired of waiting for Grant to attack."

Chapter 2

Fifteen minutes after the roar of artillery came whipping down to Savannah from Pittsburg Landing to usher in the titanic, bloody struggle of Shiloh, first great battle of the Civil War, the river bank near the Union commissary depot hummed with feverish activity.

Colonel Pollet, a dour, lanky army man in charge of the Savannah depot, came rushing down to the crowded bank where roustabouts were redoubling their efforts to load up all the moored steamboats. He spotted Horn coming down the gang-plank from the *Western Star* and stopped him with a peremptory wave of the hand.

"Horn," he said, a touch of nervous excitement oiling his voice, "I've got two barges a hundred yards downriver being loaded with ammunition. I want you to hook on to them and take them down to Pittsburg. Can you be out of here in ten more minutes?"

Horn nodded toward a number of bales and crates still waiting to be trundled aboard the *Western Star*'s freight deck. "What about the rest of that stuff?"

"Let it go," Pollet snapped. "That ammunition is more important."

"All right, Colonel," responded Horn. "I'll clear out now."

A column of infantry was winding down the hill, the men coming along at a dog trot, forage caps tilted low, rifles in hand, canteens banging against the blue-clad legs.

"You'll have to make room for half a regiment of infantry," Pollet called to Horn over his shoulder as he gestured toward the soldiers.

There was considerable confusion along the landing as soldiers began piling up there. Officers were shouting orders. Blue-clad men began to stumble up the gang-plank. Farther along the bank Horn saw Pollet talking to Kay Graham. After ward, the army man turned away and then motioned an infantry captain to march his regiment aboard *The Queen.*

Ten minutes later Colonel Pollet signalled from the bank that all the troops were aboard. The lines were cast off, Horn rang the engine room for half-speed reverse, took the wheel in his hands, and guided the *Western Star* out to midstream.

Horn tugged at the whistle cord when he slid by *The Queen* and saw Kay Graham at the wheel. A hundred yards farther on, Horn manœuvred the *Western Star* close to the bank and the two ammunition barges, one behind the other, were fastened to the stern of the packet by means of a stout hawser.

Two other packets, black smoke pouring from twin smokestacks, puffed away from the landing. Then *The Queen*, crowded to the rails with two full regiments of infantry, moved out into the middle of the river. The *Western Star* fell in a short distance to the rear.

Ahead of him *The Queen* slid out of sight around a bend in the Tennessee. Horn rang the engine room for more steam. The response was almost instantaneous. The *Western Star* forged on and slowly cut down the gap between the two boats.

He was swinging the packet around another bend in the river when the pilothouse door opened behind him. He felt the brush of cool, damp air. The vibration of moving feet along the floor told him that several men had entered the room. But he was so intent upon trying to peer through a thick screen of mist that he did not turn until the muzzle of a revolver was jammed into his back and a hard voice spoke in his ear.

"We're taking over your packet, Horn."

It was a voice that Horn had heard many times before. And now the bitter memory of it sent a ripple of shock up and down his spine. He turned slowly and found himself facing Jack Wade and two other men. All three were dressed in the uniforms of Union soldiers.

Horn glanced at the muzzle of the gun which was like a great black tunnel that seemed to grow and grow, drawing him toward destruction. His own gun was strapped around his waist, the butt nestling against his right hip. The palm of his hand grew moist and his fingers opened and closed spasmodically, tortured by the desire to go for the weapon.

Wade read that desperate intention in Horn's narrowing eyes. A malicious grin covered his olive-skinned face. He gestured to one of the bearded men behind him.

"Garvin, come up and get Horn's gun."

The man shuffled past Wade and lifted the revolver from Horn's holster. Then he stepped back warily and took up a position a few feet away. The third man remained near the door, watching the companionway that led down to the texas.

"So you're working for the Confederacy," Horn said, his voice low and even, but nevertheless distilled with rage. There was no fear in him. Rather, he was defiant and challenging. "It'll be your last job. You'll never get off this boat alive."

Wade laughed derisively. He jerked a hand at Garvin.

"Take that wheel before we ram into the bank." Then, after the Confederate spy had obeyed and sent the *Western Star* swinging back into the centre of the channel, Wade turned to Horn again.

"We got on and we'll get off again. And when we're finished with the *Western Star* Grant will be minus a few companies of infantry."

Horn said nothing, hiding the sudden concern that leaped like a hot flame within him. Wade went on:

"It's pretty easy to find Northern uniforms these days. Lots of farm kids are getting killed, and they don't all get to be buried with their soldier suits on." He laughed and the look in his cold blue eyes became darker, more unpleasant. "It was easy sneaking through the lines this morning and getting aboard in all that confusion along the landing. And it's going to be still easier to wreck this boat and the boat of that Graham gal up ahead."

Wade waited for the shock of that announcement to hit Horn. And hit him it did. His lips pulled firmly against his teeth, and taut lines appeared around his eye corners. He thought he knew what Wade planned and a horrible, sick feeling assailed his stomach.

Wade's voice droned on, confirming his suspicions.

"We're almost at Pittsburg now," he said and paused while the roar of guns beat savagely against the morning air. "*The Queen* is loaded to the railings with troops. And you're towing two ammunition barges. It shouldn't be much trouble for an experienced pilot to swing this packet around and send those barges crashing broadside into *The Queen* as she cuts in toward the landing. What do you say?"

A hot silence clamped a lid upon the pilothouse. Strain piled up until it seemed to Horn that his nerves were being scraped by the cutting edge of a knife blade.

He thought of the Union troops on his packet and of the two companies of infantry on Kay's boat—all of them unaware that at this very moment they were floating toward their doom.

Those men must not die—without a chance to fight back.

That was a conviction that grew and grew in Horn's brain. He found himself wondering how many men the Confederate had brought aboard. Probably not very many. Then it occurred to him that Wade could not risk the sound of a shot that might arouse the troops below.

That knowledge sent hot blood rushing through Horn's veins. He knew what he must do and suddenly he laughed.

There was a wild-tempered harshness in that laugh. It jerked at Wade's senses. His confidence wavered. He glanced nervously away from Horn.

And that was when Horn drove forward. Wade shifted, swinging his gun around. But Horn's swooping right arm knocked the weapon aside. With almost the same motion Horn hooked a left to Wade's chin. Wade spilled backward, fighting for balance. The spy near the door left his post and charged Horn. His gun was lifting for a shot when Wade screamed a warning.

"Don't shoot!"

There was a sudden movement behind Horn. He started to turn. Wade came in fast and hooked a glancing blow to the side of Horn's jaw. A second punch landed behind his ear. Darkness, shot through with a dazzling array of lights, whirled before his eyes.

A fist jolted his jaw again. He lashed out in self-defence. He hit empty space and felt himself falling as another heavy blow descended upon his head.

Chapter 3

He didn't even realize he was in the river until he shot, sputtering, to the surface. Waves splashed over his head. Water ran into his mouth, spilled down his throat. He gasped, fighting to suck in the precious air that would soften the agony in his lungs.

He floundered in a grey mist. The roar of artillery was sharp and clear now. There was a rush of sound somewhere nearby. It was followed by a splash that told him a stray shell had landed in the river. The increase in artillery fire could mean only one thing. The battle was in full swing and the Southern army must be driving Sherman and Prentiss out of their entrenched positions.

Horn peered through the mist, searching for the packet. It was far beyond him, its dark bulk gliding toward Pittsburg Landing two miles away. The muddy yellow shape of a thick hawser slid past his vision. One of the ammunition barges was going by.

He lashed forward, his arms cleaving the water. With a jolt of fear he noticed it was the second and last barge. He had never been a good swimmer. He was well out in midstream. If he failed to reach the barge he was finished.

A strong current caught him and whirled him backward. He redoubled his efforts, battling through a series of small waves that had been set into motion by the passage of the steamboat.

He finally fought his way clear of the treacherous eddy. But the barge was drifting past him— out of reach. He lunged on. Desperation put added power into his strokes. For just a moment it seemed that he would close the gap. He swam within one foot of the high side of the barge, then despairingly watched it elude his groping arm.

Suddenly something hard and fibrous scraped across his face. He followed through with his next stroke—and his cupped hand struck a trailing rope, gripped it instinctively, and held on.

A sensation of relief sang through him. It was pure good fortune that the barge had been carrying a length of broken towing rope, and that he'd come across it in this moment of need.

New strength flowed into his arms. He began to pull himself along the rope hauling his one hundred and eighty-five pounds through the churning Tennessee. He reached the stern of the barge and hung there a few seconds while he got back his wind.

Then he pulled himself on to the barge and staggered to his feet. Water oozed from his boots as he picked his way over stacked cases of ammunition to a narrow aisle in the middle of the barge which had been left for walking.

Halfway down the passage he was spotted by one of the crew. The man whirled from his post at the bow and came toward Horn. There was a gun in his hand.

"Hold it," the bargetender said succinctly.

"All right," said Horn and kept on walking.

The man recognized Horn's voice at the same time that he saw through the pilot's ragged appearance.

"Captain Horn!" He stopped dead, staring at Horn in amazement. "How did you get here? I thought you were—"

Horn cut in swiftly. "There's trouble on board the *Western Star*. Confederates sneaked in with

30

the Union troops. They got control of the pilot-house. I was tossed into the river after a fight."

"But how did they . . . what are they plannin' to do?"

"They aim to send the *Western Star* and these ammunition barges crashing into *The Queen* and wreck them both."

The bargeman, a stocky, blunt-jawed man with pale green eyes turned white.

"Hell, *The Queen* is loaded to the rails with infantry and—"

"Exactly," interrupted Horn again. "We've got to stop them before it's too late." Abruptly he changed the subject. "How many here besides yourself?"

"Two."

"That's enough. Come along with me. I'm going to need an extra hand or two."

The bargeman's blunt jaw seemed to stretch and grow longer.

"I'm with you, Captain."

He turned and led the way at a jogging run to the bow. Another member of the crew emerged from a small board shanty where the sleeping quarters were located. He ran toward them, then stopped as the first man ordered him back with a terse warning to alert himself for trouble.

The blunt-jawed man kept going all the way to the bow. He threw a leg over the edge of the barge and swung down to the river's surface, hanging on to the hawser that separated the two craft. Horn followed right behind him.

Hand over hand they went along the towrope until they reached the first barge. There a crewman spotted them and pulled them aboard. Once again the story was repeated and the new man was added to the ranks.

Horn flung a look out at the river and saw now that Pittsburg Landing was little more than a mile away. Time was running out. The sense of urgency was a cruel, hot knife gouging his nerves. The lives of several hundred men depended on his getting back on board the packet and stopping Jack Wade.

Rushing along the length of the barge, Horn wondered if the men in the pilothouse were watching the barges. If they were—and if he were spotted—all chance of success would be lost.

He reached the bow. The stern of the packet appeared to be empty. The few Union soldiers on board were undoubtedly clustered up front, anxiously awaiting a glimpse of the landing.

Horn didn't wait. He waved his arm at the two bargemen with him and clambered out along the towrope. His legs dragged in the water as he pulled himself hand over hand toward the steamboat. He had no thought for the weariness that filled him from head to toe. He had no thought for anything save the grim, desperate task ahead.

The stern of the packet loomed above him. He flung up a hand, found a purchase. He let go of the rope and pulled himself aboard. Then dropping to a crouch on the freight deck, he grabbed the hand of the first bargeman and hauled him up beside him. In another second the other bargeman joined them.

They went straight to the companionway and climbed to the main deck. It was deserted. They moved on up the next flight of steps.

Horn was near the top when he remembered that he had neglected to arm himself with a gun. The two bargetenders had only one revolver apiece. He shrugged and kept going to the texas.

To the right and left were a few cabins—living quarters for the captain and other officers. They were heading for the companionway that led to the pilothouse when a blue-clad man backed out of one of the cabins. He had a gun in his hand and he was talking to someone inside.

Without a word to his companions Horn moved softly along the deck toward the cabin. A sudden lull in the artillery fire brought the echo of his steps to the blue-clad man. He started to turn. Horn broke into a run. Another man crowded through the door.

Horn threw himself squarely between them. He wasn't sure if they were Union soldiers or spies. This was no time to ask questions. He had to move and move fast. And he acted on the assumption that whoever was up here on the texas had no business here. This was forbidden ground, even to soldiers.

And the minute he hit the first man with a looping right hand he knew he was right. He caught a fleeting glimpse of Dave London lying on the cabin floor, his wrists and ankles tied with heavy thongs. London was wrenching at his bonds, striving to get free.

Horn dodged the two bargemen who were battling the second spy and came at the first spy. He struck hard and fast. A hard left under the heart. Then a short, jolting right to the tip of the chin that slammed the Confederate back against the rail.

His lanky body bent backward. Suddenly he flipped over the edge and vanished. Horn whirled, ready to join the two Union bargemen. But he was not needed. The other Confederate was out cold. Blood seeped from cuts under both eyes and his jaw seemed to be dislocated.

Horn rushed to the cabin, picking up the fallen gun on the way. The two bargemen were already slashing at Dave London's bonds. At last the assistant pilot stood up.

"I'd given you up for dead, Bill," London said. He rubbed his wrists vigorously, restoring the circulation in them. "Your friend Wade is sure playin' for high stakes."

Horn grimaced angrily. He looked out at the

winding river. Again the sense of urgency went pounding through him. They were close, damnably close to the landing. Kay Graham's packet was in sight less than a hundred yards away and slowing down. They were close to the battlefield now. More and more shells came bursting over the trees to land with a dull splash in the Tennessee River.

"How many men with Wade up in the pilothouse?" Horn demanded.

"Don't know," said London tersely.

"All right. Never mind." Horn turned to one of the bargemen. "Stay at the head of the companionway and keep anyone from coming up. We'll go on to the pilothouse."

Horn hurried past the blunt-jawed man to whom he had just issued instructions and made for the companionway. He mounted the steps rapidly. Behind him came London and the other bargeman.

Horn reached the top and kicked the pilothouse door inward. He plunged inside, stepping beyond the open door. London and the other man raced through.

"Lift your hands!" called Horn, noting four blue-clad spies in the room.

Jack Wade was at the wheel. His three companions were grouped around him. Wade pivoted on his heel at the sound of Horn's voice. A ruddy streak of flame spiralled from his hand as he brought up his gun in a surprise move.

The Union bargeman uttered an agonized cry and dropped to one knee. He fired as he fell. But his bullets ploughed into the floor. The other Confederates scattered and went for their guns. Horn spilled one man with a dead-centre hit above the heart.

He fired again. Apprehension stabbed sickeningly through him when the metallic click of the hammer striking an empty cylinder came to his ears. He charged forward, throwing the gun at Wade. The Confederate tried to duck. But the arching butt slammed against the side of his head.

He reeled into Horn who came charging up to him. They met with a jarring of shoulders and thighs. Horn hit him once high on the head. Then Wade's knee shot up into the pit of his stomach. Horn's arm dropped to his sides. Wade tore himself away.

There was another flurry of shots behind Horn, a strangled shout, the thud of running boots. Then London's warning shout reached him.

"Bill, grab the wheel!"

Horn, in that one fleeting instant before he turned, saw the bargeman flat on his face with a trickle of blood welling from a hole in his neck. Two of the Confederates lay dead nearby. London, with his right shirt sleeve slowly growing red, was groping along the floor for his gun while Wade and the last remaining Confederate were fleeing toward the open door.

Torn by a desire to go after Wade and prevent him from escaping, Horn jumped back to the wheel as he felt a great shudder pass through the *Western Star.* He knew instantly that they were in shallow water and about to go aground. He planted his hands on the spokes of the wheel, rang the engine room for more steam, and heeled the boat sharply about.

Again a great trembling possessed the ship. It rocked and swayed violently as if a great wind were buffeting it. The paddle wheels churned. A muddy froth sprang out toward midchannel. There was a sudden lurch, a straining of weathered timbers, another shudder, then the boat was free and ploughing along in deeper water.

Horn glanced over his shoulder. Sweat streaked his brow and he drew a shirt sleeve across it. London was barging through the door. Horn saw him streak down the companionway.

He returned two minutes later. He met Horn's inquiring gaze and shook his head.

"Missed them. They jumped overboard and swam toward shore."

Horn's face set in hard lines.

"I'm going after Wade."

"How can you?" London demanded. He paused to stare down at the dead Confederates, then moved on to Horn's side. He held his right arm stiff and the grey pallor of his cheeks told Horn that he was in pain.

"We'll be tying up in a few minutes," Horn said, turning back to the wheel. "I'll try to pick up his trail on shore."

"No chance," said London flatly. "He'll make for the rebel lines."

"Sure and that won't be easy, either."

Chapter 4

A swarm of eager men were on hand to grab the mooring lines when the *Western Star* slid into position at the wharf with the two barges of ammunition in tow. The barge crew leaped ashore quickly to tie up their cargo. Meanwhile, the gang-plank was run out and the half company of infantry trooped ashore.

Horn and London strode on to the landing together. At once they were caught up in a bedlam of activity. Brawny muleskinners, curses streaming from their lips, lashed their sweating teams as they jockeyed their heavy army vehicles into position on the crowded landing.

Horn, tormented by the knowledge that every moment he lingered on the landing was giving Wade and his accomplices more of an opportunity to get completely away, hurried off to meet General Rawlins. The officer had moved farther along the bank, awaiting another packet which was even then steaming toward the landing.

He saw the river-boat captain and smiled. But Horn noted that it was a strained smile, without any humour or lightness in it.

"This is it, Captain," the army officer stated. "Johnston stole a march on us. He's throwing everything he has at us."

"How bad is it?" Horn demanded.

"Bad enough. Prentiss and Sherman have been forced to retreat. Johnston's game is to drive us into the river before Buell's army or Lew Wallace's division can be brought up to help." He broke off, staring beyond Horn. Then he added vehemently: "Look at those damned stragglers and deserters!"

Horn pivoted around to follow Rawlins' glance. Coming down the road that led to the bluff were a host of Union soldiers. They were a weary, bedraggled lot. Fear goaded them into a shambling run. Some of them attempted to burrow into cover under the bluff. Others, rifles dragging in their hands, tried to break away and run toward the river.

"War is hell," Rawlins muttered, "and a lot of those men are just finding it out now. Some of them are only kids. Hearing Minié balls crash all around you and seeing the man alongside you have his head taken off or lose an arm or a leg can drive a young soldier crazy with terror." He looked toward the packet that was easing up to the landing. "Got to leave you now."

"Wait!" Horn's voice was crisp and there was a diamond-hard glitter in his eyes that arrested Rawlins. "I'd like your permission to go up to the front lines."

Rawlins' ruddy face twisted in amazement.

"What for? Be glad you're back here running a river packet."

"I came near not making it—and so did those two companies of infantry that were on Miss Graham's boat."

"What's that about my packet?" demanded a voice behind Horn.

He turned and found Kay Graham had approached. General Rawlins lifted his hat. The breeze had ruffled the girl's ash-blond hair, and there was a rosy colour in her cheeks.

Briefly and impatiently Horn recounted the attempt of Wade and his men to wreck the two steamboats.

"I know for sure that Wade and one other man got away," he concluded. "They can't have gone far. They're unarmed. They'll try to reach the Confederate lines. I'd like the chance to stop them."

Rawlins shook his head.

"You're needed here to run your packet. Getting more supplies is more important than going after two spies."

"London can handle the *Western Star*," Horn said and gestured to his young aide. "I want to get Wade, General. I've known him a long time. He's dangerous. A lot of Union soldiers would be at the bottom of the Tennessee if Wade had succeeded in carrying out his plan."

Rawlins glanced sharply at Horn, sensing the iron-hard substance of the riverman—the determination to have his way in this matter.

"All right," Rawlins said with reluctance. "I think you're already too late. But go ahead and make your try. I'll send a few men along with you."

Horn began to protest. Rawlins waved him into silence.

"Don't be a complete fool," the army man said harshly. "That's no picnic over the ridge. You're much more valuable to this army as a river pilot than as a soldier. But since you're so dead set on sticking your nose into trouble I want to provide some means of getting you safely back to the landing."

He broke off to call out to a young, tough-looking sergeant who was just then passing with a detail of soldiers.

"Reardon, come over here!"

The blue-clad noncom ordered the detail to halt, then came over to join Rawlins. He saluted.

"Yes, sir?"

Rawlins explained what had happened, then added:

"Take six of your men, Sergeant, and go with Captain Horn. See if you can pick up the trail of the two Confederates—not that I have much hope of that—and bring them back. But remember this. Do not take unnecessary risks and do not cross our own lines."

Rawlins looked Horn over. The river pilot grinned tightly.

"Thanks General."

Rawlins nodded. "The sergeant will see that you get a musket. You'll need it."

Horn took a step away. Kay's hand fell on his arm, detaining him. He swung around and waited, saying nothing.

"Don't go, Bill," she murmured.

"You're wasting your time," he replied.

"Bill, I don't like to see you like this. You're crazy-mad."

He stood, big and solid and taciturn before her. His bleak, unsmiling face showed the thin, cutting edge of an uncontrollable rage.

Kay shrugged, seeing that she could not reach him, could not penetrate the stubborn wall of his resolve.

Her eyes met his in a long, strangely compelling glance. He felt something stir deep down inside him, then he thrust the feeling aside. Wildness came rushing over him and he turned away.

"Let's go," he said to the sergeant.

They had covered five hundred yards when

42

Horn suddenly veered away from the detail and moved toward the shelving bank of the river. In the wet earth close to the water's edge he saw two sets of fresh boot prints. He crouched down, following the tracks up the bank.

Farther on he came to a round depression and the prints of two hands some distance beyond. They told him that one of the fugitives had slipped and fallen to one knee while bracing himself with his hands.

Reaching the beaten trail where Reardon had paused with his troops, Horn said:

"This is it. Let's see where they went."

Reardon studied the tracks for a brief instant. A deeper gravity settled on his cheeks when he noted that they led straight over a wooded hill to the battle lines. He said nothing, however. He swung inland beside Horn and the detail fell in behind them.

They climbed the grade, the din of fighting growing stronger with each passing minute. Once in the trees they halted just long enough to be sure the trail continued to the clearing beyond. Then they went on at a fast lope across the open area and came at last to the brow of another hill.

A rattle of musketry beat hollowly against them. Below them, a quarter of a mile away, a line of blue-clad soldiers were charging across a wide field, studded at irregular intervals with huge clumps of brush. Smoke puffed from the attackers' rifles. Ahead of them, at the edge of another patch of woods, was a company of men in tattered grey and butternut brown uniforms.

Even as Horn and Reardon watched, gaps began to appear in the ranks of the Northern troops. Here and there a blue-clad figure fell forward and dropped out of sight in the weed stubble. Now, from several hidden vantage points, Confederate cannon opened up with a barrage. More and more Union soldiers pitched out of the charging line.

Suddenly the wave of Union troops broke and came running back for cover. Straight up the grade they came with the Confederates rising out of the trees to give chase. Fierce rebel yells lifted to the sky.

"We're in for it!" shouted Reardon. "They're coming this way. Drop down and get ready to fight."

Horn flung himself down behind a deadfall. He felt no excitement now that he was about to come under actual fire. Anger was still a deep drive in him and he had no room for any other emotion.

The stock of the musket slammed hard against his shoulder as he let go with a shot at a running grey-clad figure half-way down the grade. He saw the soldier take a few more reeling steps, then go twisting to earth with limp arms stretched above his head.

He reached into his pocket for another cartridge,

bit it with his strong front teeth, then rammed it home. On both sides of him now the rest of the detail was firing. The other Union troops took sudden heart at this unexpected aid, small as it was, and took up positions nearby. Soon a heavy fusillade of rifle and revolver fire raked the oncoming Grey troops. Here and there hickory shirts toppled out of the ranks, whittled down by flying lead.

Suddenly the deadfall in front of Horn erupted in a mass of broken bark and dust as a shell struck it. Debris temporarily blinded him. He rubbed his knuckles in his eyes and rolled away.

Reardon crawled to Horn's side.

"Better forget about your friend for a spell," he said huskily.

Horn nodded grimly.

"It's my damned luck."

"We're all going to need luck to get out of this," the sergeant told him.

He rolled over on his stomach, firing two shots with his pistol.

More and more grey-clad soldiers were pouring out of the woods. A wave of gunfire preceded them as they charged. The musket grew hot in Horn's fingers. Suddenly the rebels were in close. He threw down his rifle. He grabbed his pistol. A rebel lunged at him, firing as he came. Horn dropped him with a shot from the hip. He turned to face another enemy soldier rushing in from the side. He felt his gun kick in his palm and he knew he had fired. Then a heavy blow struck his side and he felt himself falling through a great, endless black void.

Chapter 5

Horn's eyes flipped wearily open. The lids seemed heavy and weighted. There were trees around him and men in blue. And all the while there was that constant feeling of motion. Then for a brief, lucid interval he saw that he lay on a crude canvas litter. The straight, narrow back of a soldier loomed in front of him, hard-knuckled hands gripping the stretcher poles. Behind him he sensed another soldier, though he couldn't bring himself to turn and make sure.

Pain was a searing iron in his side. It played on his nerves with violent, nagging fingers. His vision dimmed. The blackness rolled in again. A great wave of it reached for him and sucked him out and away.

When he regained consciousness once more daylight had faded from the sky and a hard, slashing rain was pelting the land. Smoking lanterns broke the gloom around him. He lay on the ground now in the lee of a granite bluff near the landing. Other dark, motionless shapes sprawled inertly in the shadows. Out of those shadows a hoarse voice cried for water.

Two bandsmen appeared out of the darkness and moved toward him. They placed a stretcher on the ground, hefted him on to it, then carried him down toward the landing. In motion again the pain in his side was renewed with savage vigour.

The bandsmen transported Horn inside the huge frame building where a pitifully small group of doctors had been labouring for hours in a frantic effort to patch up the wounded.

Horn felt a cold perspiration seeping out of his pores. He was on a pine table now. An orderly ripped open his shirt, drew down his trousers, exposing the raw, bullet-gashed skin.

Horn saw the shadow of a long arm on the wall beside him. The arm grew longer, stretching out to an interminable length and at last ending in a sharp, curving prong. He turned and saw a surgeon come up to the table. He knew, then, that he was next.

Rain drummed against the roof. A wind sprang up, shouldering roughly against the frame walls of the building. Yonder, near the door, two officers were talking. Snatches of their conversation drifted to Horn as the orderly pressed a drink of brandy to his lips.

"Too bad about Prentiss . . . surrendered with twenty-five hundred men . . ."

"He held on as long as he could . . . four hours."

"Yeah. Without him and Wallace and Hurlbut we'd all be in the middle of the Tennessee . . ."

"But can we continue to hold on?"

"There's a good chance. . . . Buell's advance is moving in now."

That was all Horn heard for a little while. Brandy was poured into his wound. He felt it burn down deep into his vitals. Then came the prick of the scalpel, the slick flash of razor-edged steel slicing through his flesh. He hovered on the edge of unconsciousness. A red haze whirled in front of his eyes growing progressively darker. Little devils of agony thrusting and gouging at his side swept away the filmy curtain that obscured his vision.

Then, abruptly, it was over and they were carrying him out into the night and the pouring rain. The boots of the bandsmen who held the stretcher made hideous, sucking noises in the mud as they trudged up the hill to the bluff.

Horn slept fitfully, his slumber disturbed by wild dreams, by the persistent ache of his wound, and by the never-ending tumult of activity behind the Union lines.

At last, near dawn, he was removed, with other casualties, to the deck of one of the river packets. There, as the grey day moved steadily along news began to drift in from the battlefront.

Al Johnston, leading his Confederate forces in

an assault against "The Hornet's Nest," a Union strong point, was struck in the leg by a Minié ball. Not realizing that an artery had been severed, the general stayed with his troops—and died thirty minutes later.

Beauregard, second in command, had taken over. But by morning the opportunity to take the offensive was whipped out of Beauregard's hands.

Grant drew together his scattered brigades and joined to them the fresh divisions of Buell as well as that of Lew Wallace (who had got lost the day before and taken the wrong road to Shiloh) and set into motion a vicious counter-attack that eventually pushed Beauregard's army all the way back to Corinth.

Late that afternoon Horn became aware that he was on *The Queen* when he saw Kay Graham come aboard, stop to talk to a burly man he recognized as Tug Wilson, her first mate, then rows of wounded men, pausing here and there to drop a smile and a word of cheer.

She was almost upon Horn before she noticed him.

"Bill!" she gasped. For a moment all her cool composure vanished and she knelt beside him. "I—I didn't know. I've been waiting and wondering if . . ." She broke off, reddening a trifle as she saw how intently he was regarding her. "Is it bad, Bill?"

He grinned. "I always thought those Johnny

Rebs could shoot straight. Guess I was wrong. Got me in the side." He reached for her hand.

For the past twenty-four hours he had been absorbed by the heat and excitement of battle. Now a different—a pleasurable—excitement held him. That this reaction was produced by Kay, whose presence was such a compelling force beside him, he quickly acknowledged to himself.

He pulled her toward him. She was yielding to the pressure, her face drawing nearer to his, when she saw his expression alter. She stiffened and he dropped her hand. He was no longer smiling.

It happened just like that. One moment he was in the grip of desire that was like a powerful drug impelling him toward her. The next moment black memories came crowding into his mind and he seemed to be looking at her over a high, insurmountable wall.

His glance slid uncomfortably away from her. When he looked again the smile was still on her lips, but it was no longer warm and personal. Nothing else had changed in her face. When at last she spoke again her voice was as cool and contained as it had ever been.

"You didn't find Wade." It was a statement more than a question.

"No," he said and told her briefly of the unsuccessful chase. "We were too late." He was angry and disappointed and could not easily hide it. "He's one up on me."

"You mean two up, don't you?" There was an edge to her laugh.

Their eyes met sharply like the points of matched rapiers. All at once they were strangers again.

"Leave Irene out of it," he said.

"Who said anything about Irene?"

"You didn't mean anything else."

She regarded him closely, her eyes grave and questioning.

"The hurt's still there, isn't it? It's never gone away."

Horn couldn't stand the pity in her glance. It seemed to him also, that there was a subtle overtone of amusement in her manner.

"There must be other men on this packet you could pay a visit to," he said with a savage distinctness. He saw several wounded figures nearby shift and turn their attention his way. He went recklessly, angrily on: "Well, what are you waiting for? Why don't you go?"

Kay caught an uneven, startled breath. Her cheeks lost colour.

"All right, Bill. I'll go." The words came from her, flat and sharp. She started to walk away. Then, some inner compulsion brought her fully around to him again. "That was a crazy thing you did—going off into a scrap after one man and getting a bullet for your trouble. But it was kind of magnificent, too." She paused and her

51

voice dropped a notch. "I had to tell you that."

Horn made no answer. Not a muscle in his face moved. Only his eyes steadily watched her—wary and suspicious of irony.

By the time he realized her praise had been sincere she had turned and was walking away. For many a day afterward he wondered what would have happened if he had called her back, then.

Some devil of pride clamped a lid on his lips. He stared at her tall, straight back as she moved straight and fast away from him—through the windrows of wounded and on out of sight.

Late that night *The Queen* pulled away from Pittsburg Landing, its decks crowded with blue-clad Missourians, bound for homes and hospitals in St. Louis. And just a few hundred yards behind it steamed the *John J. Roe* with a host of wounded men from Indiana, their destination far-off Evansville and other points in the Hoosier state.

Kay did not appear again that night. Horn imagined her up in the pilothouse, her strong slender hands gripping the wheel, her keen eyes searching out the elusive channel of the Tennessee.

Chapter 6

Late morning sunlight streamed through the dust and rain-spotted windows of Bill Horn's hotel room. Shiloh was three week's behind him. He had been out of bed for eight days now and his strength, bringing with it a boundless energy, was beginning to flow back to his muscles.

He moved to the window, flung it roughly open. A warm breeze flowed in. It rippled the faded pink curtains. He thrust the curtains out of the way. Street noises reached him. The rumble of wagon wheels, the snap of a muleskinner's whip, the chatter of young children, and the pounding of their feet in the dust.

Down at the end of the street he could see the landing and directly beyond it the brown rush of the Mississippi. Packets were tied up along the levee. Out in midstream a log raft floated by, a brawny logger leaning on the heavy locust sweep in the stern.

As Horn's attention swung back to the hotel he saw a black carriage, drawn by a fine pair of bays, drive away from the entrance. He looked for some sign of the occupants along the board walk and concluded that they had entered the hotel lobby.

A light tap on the door startled him. He turned and called:

"Come in."

The door opened wide and Kay Graham stood there. She was dressed in blue, as always. Every curl of her ash-blond hair was in place. She moved serenely into the room, the crinkled blue crepe of her dress swirling about her hips with each rhythmic, flowing step.

"I just got back from a short run to Boonville," she said and advanced to the window. "How are you, Bill?"

There was no strain, no discomfort in her manner. For one brief moment he thought he saw an expression of concern in her eyes. But when he looked again her glance was measured and even. Friendly enough, but impersonal.

"I'm all right," he said. "About ready to take to the river again."

"Going to make the Fort Benton run this season?"

He nodded. "Dave London has been handling things for me. There's a cargo of lumber waiting for me at Yankton."

He didn't sound very enthusiastic. Even the prospect of activity—the chance of taking up his old stand in the pilothouse of the *Western Star*— should have brought him an element of pleasure. Obviously it did not. And suddenly Kay knew the reason why. He felt left out of things. He would be remembering Shiloh now—the roar of guns, the rumble of caissons, the mud and the rain, the violent sweep of battle, the talking and shouting of men fighting side by side for the same cause.

He would be thinking that was all over—for him. The fight was still going on, in Tennessee and in Virginia, but he was no longer a part of it.

Kay had a way of reading him, and she read him now with an understanding tempered by warm amusement. But she was wise enough in the ways of men not to let this amusement show in her face. He was a proud and sensitive man and he was carefully watching her.

"Don't be too sure about Yankton," she said.

There was truculence in the way Horn lifted his shoulders and in the way his words came back at her.

"Why not?"

She was carrying a soft blue leather bag by a strap on one arm. She opened a gold clasp and dipped a hand inside. She removed a letter and passed it to him.

"Take a look at that," she said.

He hesitated, regarding her with a slight frown.

"What are you waiting for?" she demanded impatiently. "It's addressed to you."

"I see that," he answered quietly. "How did you come by this?"

"I stopped off at the levee on my way from *The Queen*. I thought you might be on your packet.

Dave London was there. He had this letter. It had just come in on the mail packet from the Ohio River and the East. You'll notice it's postmarked Washington."

"Maybe you know what it says."

Kay ignored the hard bite of his words.

"I can guess," she murmured.

He lowered his head, slit the envelope with a fingernail, and drew forth a single sheet of paper carrying the official seal of the government. As he read the message a strange excitement brought a rush of blood to his face.

He looked up, at last. His voice, when he spoke, had a ring to it.

"I'll be going to Yankton," he said, "but not for lumber."

Kay nodded. "For Sioux instead?"

Horn was smiling. But now his mouth tightened quickly.

"How did you know?"

She delved into her bag again and drew out another letter.

"I received one of those letters, too." She laughed. There was excitement in the laugh. "Looks like we'll be seeing each other in Yankton. Washington is worried about the Sioux Indians."

Horn glanced down at the letter, then up at Kay again.

"This is right from the Assistant Secretary of War. The Sioux are on a rampage in Montana and

Dakota Territory. Seems they've found out the government's got a war on its hands and have decided it's a good time to bust out and raid the settlements."

"That's not all they're doing," Kay added. "Down at the landing I ran into Gus Anderson, captain and pilot of the *North Wind*. He's just in from a trip to the Yellowstone. He says that a band of Sioux opened fire with rifles on his packets from the bluffs a few miles below Fort Union."

Horn forgot the tight feeling of enmity that usually swirled between them as his mind ranged eagerly into the future.

"Maybe we will see some action, after all," he murmured. "If the War Department thinks it necessary to send an expedition into Dakota, the Sioux must be really massing their lodges for a major campaign against the upper river settlements."

"In a way, you can't blame the Sioux," Kay said. "They've got a raw deal from Washington. Every time the government gives them a strip of territory to live and hunt in, along come a bunch of white men to push them farther westward."

The corners of Horn's eyes puckered in thoughtful concentration.

"You're right about that, Kay. But I don't reckon there's any man living who could have stopped the things that have happened and are still going to happen. The Sioux are going to fight to hold their land. And in so doing, they'll be killing white settlers and burning homes. The government's answer to that is soldiers. That's where we come in."

Kay walked to the window. She stared down at the street with its clutter of carriages, wagons, and men. Then she put her back to the window. The morning sunlight behind her emphasized the lithe slimness of her body. There was a lusty strength to this girl and she had a degree of vitality that always astonished Horn.

"Well, Washington picked the best packets and the best pilots for the job of keeping its Indian fighters supplied." Kay laughed when she said that, but one look at the determined set of her jaw, the eager brightness of her eyes, told him she was completely serious.

It brought him back to reality. It reminded him that Kay was a rival of his in the river trade—and a shrewd, hardheaded rival at that. He must, therefore, be on his guard with her.

"You seem very sure about that," he said rather tartly.

She looked straight at him in a way that was a challenge. Not the coquettish challenge of a woman using her charms to fence with a man, but the direct defiance of one man throwing the weight of his will against another man. It was that harsh and thoroughly recognizable.

"Anybody in St. Louis will tell you I don't make

idle talk. You're the best on the Missouri—or so they tell me." The bite of acid was in her words. "I'm the best on the Mississippi. And give me one trip on your Big Muddy and I'll take *The Queen* into any place you take the *Western Star.*"

He laughed humourlessly.

"If the Sioux happen to hole up in the Little Missouri country the army will probably expect us to take them up the Yellowstone. What then?"

Kay's answer came quickly and without hesitation.

"I've heard the Yellowstone is too swift and shallow for steamboats," she said. "But if the troops and supplies have to go that way I'll take *The Queen* through—even if I have to grasshopper the entire length of the river."

She glared at Horn, suddenly hating his man's pride, his smug assurance. She walked away from the window. In front of the discoloured mirror she paused to straighten her feathery blue hat. She was in the shadows in the room's far corner when a light tap sounded on the door.

Before Horn could answer the summons the knob turned and the door swung open. He had started around the foot of the iron bed. Now he stopped as if his feet had become rooted to the floor. His face was white. Somewhere deep inside him a heavy pulse began its uneven throbbing. But not once did he take his eyes away from the girl in the doorway.

She was small and dark haired with creamy tan skin. Her smooth, fine-drawn features held a note of uncertainty, but her lips were close to a smile.

Then she ran straight to Horn, calling his name in a strained, husky voice that stabbed through him with a haunting familiarity. Somehow she was in his arms and she was kissing him.

"Bill," she whispered, her hands clinging to him with a touch that was possessive and almost greedy. "It's been so long." There was a pleading urgency in her green, long-lashed eyes.

There was a numbness in him. He couldn't think. He couldn't feel. All he said was, "Irene," and this seemed to come from some place far removed from him.

"Bill, I've been away," she went on, talking breathlessly as if they were both under a spell that must not be shattered. "I just heard to-day about you—I mean about what happened at Shiloh. Oh, Bill—you might have been killed."

"Since when have you started worrying about him again?" Kay asked sharply, advancing toward the window.

Irene Nostrum pivoted. Her liquid green eyes narrowed. Her round, small face stiffened.

"What are you doing here?" she demanded.

Kay laughed, though her lips barely moved.

"Irene, you surprise me. You're a woman and you can't guess that?"

These two women had never liked each other

and their antagonism was never more apparent than at this moment. Irene, petite and soft and entirely feminine, secretly resented Kay's conspicuous success in a rough world dominated by men, her obvious strength, her sharp tongue. And Kay, always direct and frank, was suspicious of Irene's softness, her cloying sweetness and preening in the presence of men.

"Go back to your steamboat," Irene snapped, a spasm of jealousy going through her. "Bill isn't your kind of man."

Again Kay laughed. But her eyes were cold and unfriendly.

"I presume you mean he is your kind of man. God help him if it's true."

Irene's small hands clenched. She turned from Horn, took a step toward Kay. Anger was a hot, wicked flame in her eyes. Kay stood altogether still, her arms at her sides.

"Go ahead," she said. "I'm waiting."

The cool competence of her stopped Irene. Kay sensed that the other girl longed to sink her fingernails into her cheeks, yet didn't dare.

A tight, uncomfortable silence fell upon the room. Kay gave Horn a long, direct look. He was frowning as he met her glance and a struggle seemed to be going on behind his eyes.

"Good-bye, Bill," Kay said. "I'll be seeing you in Yankton. Take care of yourself." She added softly to the other girl: "You too, Irene."

She walked past them, her body straight and tall and graceful. The door closed quietly.

Irene shrugged, brought a smile back to her face. She came over to Horn. There was a sudden haggard look about him that puzzled her.

"What is it, Bill?" she asked.

"There's no going back—for us," he said at last.

A slender vein along her white throat began to beat.

"Bill, you don't mean that."

She pressed against him. She kissed him again, clinging to him, her mouth hungry and demanding.

Bill Horn felt the stir of old, remembered pleasure. Heat was moving in his blood. He lifted his hands to her arms, pushed her away.

"It's no use, Irene," he said and hoped she would not detect the doubt in his voice.

"It isn't true," she insisted. "It isn't."

She had been a bright, searing flame in his life. Theirs had been a wild, sweet courtship. To him she had been all that he had ever hoped to find in a woman. Then the break had come and he had seen behind the smooth, soft mask of her beauty to the shrewd, faithless core of her.

For him the flame had gone out, then. Perhaps he expected too much of a woman. There had never been anyone but Irene. He had been sure there would never be anyone but her. Wade and Irene together had helped to kill that notion.

And so he had put her behind him. He had turned hard and bitter. He had lost himself in the world of men—in the rough company of loggers and raftsmen and river pilots.

He was angry that Irene should still have the capacity to stir his emotions. The wildness and the sweetness of her were terribly real and terribly vivid and they blurred that long, dim interval of pain and bitterness.

Because he was conscious of her close scrutiny and wanted to still the leaping surge of his emotions, he took refuge in anger.

"Did you think you could come back at any time you pleased and pick up where we left off?" he asked.

Irene stepped back from him. Her breathing quickened.

"Bill," she said, "you've a perfect right to be angry. I'm sorry. I've so much to make up to you. Jack Wade—that was all a mistake. I knew it— soon after you left St. Louis that time."

She was looking straight at him, her eyes hurt and a little wistful. She seemed altogether lovely —and defenceless.

He felt the strong tug of her nearness. He wanted to kiss her red, upturned mouth. But he steeled himself.

"Maybe they didn't tell you that Wade tried to blow up *The Queen* and the *Western Star*."

She nodded. "I know. But that was war." The

darkening expression on Horn's face made her hasten to add: "I'm not defending Jack or myself. I've been wrong. Isn't there a—a chance for us?"

Her eyes were very green. They were close to his. There were tiny lines around them. He tried to read them and couldn't.

"You're fighting me," she said with shrewd insight. "I can tell."

They were interrupted by the rush of footsteps coming down the hallway. Knuckles rapped on the door.

Horn called, "Come in."

Irene drew back as the door opened to admit Dave London. The thin, wiry assistant pilot looked excited.

"Bill, I just met Kay down on the levee and—" He broke off as he noticed Irene. His weathered features turned a little darker. He nodded to the girl. "Hello, Irene."

She acknowledged his greeting with a meagre smile, sensing his dislike. London ignored her after that.

"Kay told me about that government proposition," he went on. "It sure listens good and I'm glad we'll be back in harness. Reckon you'll want me to get the *Western Star* ready for service. Just a few minor engine repairs and we'll be set."

London's enthusiasm communicated itself to Horn. The prospect of the coming trip upriver was a boon to his spirits. He momentarily forgot about Irene.

"I'll leave everything to you, Dave," he said. "General Dale Macy, commander of the 5th Cavalry, is at Yankton and from the tone of that Washington note he wants us there as soon as we can make it."

"To-day is Tuesday," London murmured. "You can figure on Thursday morning."

"Good."

London grinned and shuffled toward the door.

"Maybe we'll see some action before the summer is over," he said. "If we can't shoot Confederates we can maybe get ourselves a couple Sioux warriors."

A certain grim earnestness came into Horn's cheeks.

"You can count on plenty of hell up in Dakota," he stated. "The Sioux have been threatening to make real trouble for two–three years. This time I've a feeling we'll get it."

"Suits me fine," replied London.

He walked to the door, gave Irene a curt nod, and stepped out into the corridor. Irene waited until his footsteps had died away before speaking.

"You've hired out the *Western Star* to the government?"

"Yes. The Sioux are raising hob all along the Missouri and especially in Dakota Territory. Macy evidently has orders to take the 5th Cavalry in there and smash them."

"And your job is to keep the troops supplied?"

"Right."

"Kay's boat has been hired, too?"

"Yes." He saw the tightening line of her mouth and felt impelled to explain. *"The Queen* and the *Western Star* are about the two fastest and sturdiest packets in service. Besides, they both have a shallow draft—an important consideration when the river runs low during midsummer."

Irene considered that information a few seconds. Then she stepped close to him, her eyes shining with the brightness of an idea.

"Bill, you can take me along," she suggested. "That way we can be together."

Her soft glance was like a warm caress. Horn was conscious of the slow twitching of his shoulder muscles. There was sweat in the palms of his hands.

"No. Not this time, Irene."

"I know," she said hotly. "You're afraid. You don't trust yourself with me."

He saw the thin core of her thinking. She was restless and bored. It was enough for her that she wanted him. She was impatient of obstacles.

"This will be no picnic," Horn told her. "It's war—another kind of war. Dakota during the next few months will be no place for women."

"What about Kay?" she asked, her eyes dark.

"You can answer that yourself. The army needs good river pilots. Kay is one of the best."

Irene bit her lip. She was losing Horn. And she was losing her plea.

"Dale Macy is my cousin. Did you know that? He'll let me go. Just take me to Yankton."

Horn ran a hand through his unruly black hair. He shook his head and his deep-socketed eyes regarded her gravely.

"No passengers, Irene. That goes. I'm sorry."

"All right, Bill." She held out her hand and he took it. "But promise me you'll visit me to-morrow. At the Palmer House."

He nodded curtly, but without any intention of keeping the appointment.

Chapter 7

Eleven days later the *Western Star* and *The Queen* steamed up to the landing at Yankton, the territorial capital. A large crowd, drawn by the spreading rumours of an impending Indian campaign, was on hand. Eager hands grasped the mooring lines and made them fast. The gang-planks were run out and Kay and Bill came down to meet amid the confusion of bales and cases and barrels that lined the bank.

"Where's Irene?" Kay asked, a low mocking note in her voice.

Horn frowned. "Back in St. Louis, I reckon."

"So you didn't change your mind."

"Let's forget about her," he said impatiently. "We've got important business here. Don't you remember?"

Kay gave him a long, cool, appraising look. Then she smiled faintly.

"I'm ready if you are."

For just a moment Kay had been personal. Yet even in that short interval there was a subtle shading of satiric humour in her words. And her bold eyes seemed to be laughing at him. Now, walking up the long hill toward the scatter of frame buildings that comprised the town Kay was brisk and businesslike. She matched Horn's great stride apparently without effort. Vivid colour tinted her cheeks and she was absorbing the rough sights and sounds of Yankton with a bright, alert interest.

Three weeks had gone by since General Dale Macy had ridden in from Fort Leavenworth with five companies of the 5th Cavalry and set up this temporary camp above the town. The blue-clad troopers had brought new life to Yankton. Saloons and stores had done a booming business. Day after day the peal of bugles sounding reveille, assembly, dress drill, retreat, tattoo, and taps had mingled with the hoot of steamboat whistles down on the river, the chanting of roustabouts, and the rumble of freight wagons.

Reaching the edge of the broad parade ground, Kay and Horn drew to a halt as the trumpeters, standing straight and still beneath the furling flag a short distance from headquarters tent, blew the sharp clear notes for drill call.

Troopers immediately began hurrying from their tents. Orderlies ran from the open corrals beyond camp, leading groups of horses. The company streets were alive with men rushing in every direction, some fumbling with sabre belts, others slamming campaign hats into rakish positions on their thick-haired heads or adjusting side-arms holsters.

A towering, black-haired man on a great black horse rode out to the edge of the parade ground. He sat stiffly in the saddle, watching the companies wheel and march before him. After five minutes or so the officers of each company pivoted about and trotted toward the commanding officer of the regiment. They paused before him, hands slicing quickly and smartly up to their foreheads. The regimental commander returned the salute, then watched them turn and ride back.

Kay, turning away from the spectacle, saw Horn's sombre grey eyes still fastened on the uniformed figures dissolving along the edges of the parade. There was a bright glint of excitement in his face. The colour, the grand sweep of motion, the clank of sabres, the shrill call of officers' voices, the pageant of men working and toiling together as a unit was like a rich wine in his blood. It lifted his spirits, filled him with a powerful longing—and with an indefinable sadness because he could not be a part of it.

She reached out and touched his arm.

"That's what you'd like to be doing, isn't it?" she asked gently.

"Yes," he answered. "How did you know?"

His glance came slowly around to her. For just this moment her eyes were not impersonal. They were warm and soft and filled with understanding.

"I know men—and I know you," she said. "This life—the dangers, the sweat and the toil, the drinking and the laughter, the smell of horses, the call of a trumpet—fills a need in some men. You're one of those men."

Horn looked at Kay with a new respect. Her ability to see through him, to reach deeply into the inner springs of his being had amazed him more than once. Now he felt drawn a little closer to her. A sort of quiet ease came between them.

"I'd give a lot to be with these troopers," he said. " Much as the river has always been a part of my life, with the war on and so many things needing to be done, the army is one place where a man forgets about himself. He becomes a number, a uniform—a minor cog in a fine fighting machine."

Horn's voice was deadly serious and Kay answered him in an equally grave manner.

"Every time you make a trip to Fort Benton at the wheel of the *Western Star*—or even while you're here at Yankton to help supply an expedition in the field—you're fighting the same fight those men in blue are fighting. The only difference between you and them is that you wear no uniform."

Horn didn't answer, and so in silence they moved along the parade until they reached headquarters tent. An orderly pushed aside the brown flap and stepped into the narrow ribbon of dust that served as a street.

"Will you tell General Macy that Miss Graham and Bill Horn have arrived and would like a few moments of his time?" Horn requested.

The orderly let his admiring eyes settle on Kay, then nodded pleasantly and turned back inside the tent. He reappeared at once.

"The general will see you," he said. "Won't you step this way?"

He held the flap open so that Kay could step inside. Horn followed her, blinking his eyes in the dim flicker of lamplight. There was a rough army cot in one corner. Beside it was a plain board table surrounded by several home-made chairs. A smoking kerosene lamp stood on the table, and a second lamp rested on the edge of the cot.

Dale Macy was a tall man, slightly round-shouldered with a great shock of black hair, snapping black eyes, and long sideboards. Horn had a tremendous respect for the man, knowing him to be an experienced Indian campaigner, a shrewd judge of officers and utterly fearless in battle.

He shifted some maps and other papers on the table, then came around and moved one of the spare chairs near Kay.

"Please be seated, Miss Graham," he said and waited for Kay to take the chair. Then he went back behind the table. "I am glad you both accepted the government's offer," he resumed. "God knows the cavalry is headed for plenty of trouble in the next few months in mighty rough country. I don't have to tell you how difficult it is to feed an army in the wilderness. That's why I've placed so much emphasis on getting boats that can follow me up the Yellowstone, the Powder, the Little Big Horn—if it proves necessary to catch up with the Sioux."

"I take it this will be an all-out campaign, then?" Horn asked.

Macy's lips quivered in a dry, mirthless smile.

"That's what Washington is calling it," he said. "But they've given me only seven companies of cavalry to wipe out more than fifteen hundred Sioux warriors."

Macy looked toward the entrance of the tent as he heard the orderly speaking in a low voice.

"Go right in. The general is expecting you."

Horn swung around. His eyes widened in amazement when he saw Irene Nostrum, flanked by three lieutenants, come in from the company street. She looked flushed and happy.

"Surprise," she murmured.

"How did you get here?" Horn demanded.

"There are other packets making the run from St. Louis to Yankton," she told him. Then turning to Kay, she added, "And how are you, Kay dear?"

"Well, Irene," said Macy, "you seem to have gathered my best young officers around you."

Irene made a face at him, but Kay could see that she was pleased. The small, dark-haired girl, conscious of the admiring glances of the three lieutenants, preened herself before them. She favoured each of them with a shy glance in which there was just the right amount of coquetry.

"I gather you have both met Irene, who is my cousin by marriage," Macy said to Kay and Bill Horn. "The gentlemen with her are Lieutenants Lowell, Breadon, and Husking, commanding companies A, D, and E respectively of the 5th Cavalry."

After the introductions were acknowledged by everyone, the general went on talking, his words being directed primarily to Horn.

"I've asked my line officers here so that you could meet them since you will be working with them during the coming weeks. Also, they are fully aware of the scope of the campaign and the risks involved.

"The Sioux have been making plenty of trouble along the Missouri, as I've already indicated in my letter. But they are not our only problem. There are also the Jayhawkers."

"Jayhawkers?" Kay repeated, her face bright with interest.

"Renegades," explained Macy. "Some of them are deserters from our own armies, others from the Confederates. They have been going on private raids in the Shenandoah Valley of Virginia, killing and pillaging everything in sight. Sometimes they masquerade in Union uniforms; other times they pose as Confederate soldiers. Lately some of them have shifted operations to the upper Mississippi and Missouri, attacking river packets with valuable cargo.

"Just ten days ago I received a report that Jayhawkers had sacked a small steamboat bound downriver from Fort Benton and carrying a hundred thousand dollars in gold."

"Gold!" ejaculated Horn. "Has there been a new strike?" He looked closely at the cavalry commander. "Miners have been pulling gold out of the country south of Three Forks ever since 1852, but there's been no real bonanza."

"From the rumours drifting in lately it appears that they've finally struck it rich in Bannock, near the Continental Divide," said Macy. "That complicates matters for the government. We know there are Confederate spies operating in Dakota Territory, stirring up the Sioux to revolt. With gold beginning to pour down here from Fort Benton as Bannock booms, those Confederate agents will do all they can to grab some of those shipments for Jeff Davis."

"Have you any idea who is behind the Jayhawkers?" Horn asked, a note of bleak expectancy in his query.

Macy planted both palms on the rough table and leaned forward.

"One name has been mentioned," he said. "The packet which was attacked and run aground with its cargo of gold near the mouth of the Knife River put up a fight with the Jayhawkers. The pilot, who was wounded but got away and was picked up by another downriver boat, said that the renegades were led by a former Missouri River man—Jack Wade."

"Ah!" The sound was a gusty outpouring of breath from Horn's lungs. "I expected that."

There was a sudden consuming fire in him. It shook him up, drove him forward in a burst of nervous energy. It was a wildness that made its indirect impact upon every man in the tent. Macy looked up.

"I thought you'd be interested," the general said. "Especially after Shiloh."

Rage thickened Horn's words when next he spoke.

"My friend Wade covers a lot of ground. But jayhawking is the kind of thing he's cut out for. Some day we'll meet again and I'll settle my little account with him."

Then Horn reverted to the subject of the forthcoming campaign.

"You have a plan of attack mapped out, General?"

Macy shook his head.

"Nothing so elaborate as that. The main job of the 5th Cavalry will be to lick Chief Wild Horse and his Sioux outlaws. If we run into some Jayhawkers that'll be all to the good. But I've got hardly enough men to handle those redskins without wasting time scouting all over Dakota in search of roving bands of white renegades.

"Fort Union will serve as our supply base—unless the movement of the Indians forces me to establish another base. I expect we'll find them somewhere along the Little Missouri. But no matter where they are I intend to smoke them out."

Macy paused a moment, prodded the papers on the table with the blunt edges of his fingers.

"I'm taking five river packets in all," he resumed. "The *Western Star* and *The Queen* will carry the three companies of cavalry plus food and ordnance supplies. The other three will be used to transport the horses, grain, and extra food supplies for the troops.

"At Fort Union the three extra packets will be sent back to Yankton. Your boat, Captain Horn, and the boat of Miss Graham will be retained to follow the march of the cavalry as far as possible."

"Good enough," said Kay, suddenly taking the initiative. "When do you plan to leave Yankton?"

"Day after to-morrow," replied Macy. "All the supplies are ready."

"We'll start loading this afternoon," cut in Horn. "You'll find us ready when you are."

"That goes for me, too," added Kay.

Macy nodded, a grim smile on his tight lips.

"That will be all, then. And once again, thank you for your co-operation. I appreciate it."

"Don't thank me," said Horn. "I want a crack at those Sioux—and maybe at my friend, Wade."

"The Sioux you can definitely count on," said Lieutenant Breadon and turned his back on Horn, moving to Irene's side and guiding her toward the tent flap as they all prepared to leave.

Chapter 8

By the time Horn got outside Irene and Breadon were at the edge of the parade. They had left the other two cavalry officers behind. Lowell and Husking paused to shake hands with Horn. Then they gallantly doffed their campaign hats and said good-bye to Kay.

Horn walked on, planning to catch up to Irene. But when neither she nor Breadon turned he slowed down. There was a tight look on his face when Kay moved alongside him.

"You're a little late, Bill," she said.

"Yeah." He bit the word off.

"A few brass buttons might help."

Horn turned to her, his features darkening. Then he saw the languid smile on her lips and knew she was secretly amused.

The spasm of anger passed. For a reason he could not name he felt a bond of friendship with Kay. Although he was not willing to admit it, he somehow knew that he had been wrong in blaming her for the sinking of the *Western Star* when Wade had been in her employ.

"Shall we go to the landing?" he asked quietly. "We both have work to do."

"Yes," she agreed. "And it's work that won't wait."

At the gang-plank of *The Queen* Kay merely touched Horn's arm, smiled briefly, and passed on up to the deck of her packet. He lifted his cap and remained utterly still for a few seconds while he watched her walk gracefully away. Then he tramped on to the *Western Star.*

In the middle of the afternoon General Macy sent a detail of men down to the landing. A brawny sergeant, in charge of quartermaster supplies, commanded the detail. He reported to Horn; then, along with a portion of the *Western Star*'s crew, they went to a warehouse which had been taken over by the 5th Cavalry.

Boxes of ammunition, both for the standard Colt revolvers and the Springfield carbines, were stacked along a section of one wall. These were carried to the deck of Horn's packet and carefully shored up to avoid shifting their position.

Shortly before the bugles blew retreat at the camp the sergeant took his detail of soldiers back to the plateau above the town. Later, from the high texas deck Horn listened to the strident notes of the bugles floating out across the river and watched the lowering of the colours from the crude flagpole which had been set up at the far end of the parade.

Afterward, going toward the bow of his boat he was startled to hear the scuff of footsteps behind him. Dark as it was, with only the glow of the pitch-burning deck lamps to diffuse the thick-running shadows, Horn instantly recognized Irene.

She came toward him, her slender willowy body swaying provocatively. She said softly:

"Hello, Bill. I haven't seen you all afternoon."

She stood directly before him, her face a white, up-turned oval in the darkness. There was a subtle fragrance to her hair. A strand of it softly flicked against the skin of his blunt jaw.

"I was here," he told her shortly.

She understood the unsaid things that were implied in his laconic reply, but chose to ignore them. Deftly she changed the subject.

"I'm going to Fort Union with you, Bill."

Her announcement came with a jog of surprise.

"Not if I've got anything to say about it," Horn retorted.

A look of serene contentment covered her features.

"That's just it. You have nothing to say."

"I'm still captain of the *Western Star*," he snapped.

"But Macy is commander of the expedition and you and your packet have hired out to work for him." She smiled archly up at him. "If he says I go, I go. And he's already said yes."

Horn reached out and placed his hands firmly on her shoulders. He spoke with grim earnestness.

"Irene, why in God's name do you want to go along? We're fighting a war and there'll be no place for you once Macy's cavalry swing into the field."

"I've no intention of riding with the troops. I can stay on the *Western Star* or at Fort Union."

He shook her gently, his fingers digging into her soft, rounded flesh.

"Either way you're running a risk. Don't you know that the Sioux raided Fort Union twice

80

during the winter and they've already fired on several packets. What's to prevent them from doing it again—while you're there?"

"Bill," she said in a chiding tone, "you're as bad as Cousin Dale. He didn't want me to go at first —until I talked to him. I promised I'd stay out of his way and not interfere. But I *am* going. As for the Sioux, the cavalry will take care of them easily enough."

A feeling of irritation slugged through Horn. He had a view of the narrow, selfish side of Irene's nature and it wasn't a pleasing sight. She had no thought for the tremendous dangers involved, for the sturdy young men who would later dash into battle and never return. This was an adventure—a gay and reckless undertaking and she found a vicarious enjoyment in the knowledge that she had forced her way in.

"All right," he said, his hands dropping away from her in a gesture of resignation. "I guess it's all settled."

Irene made no move to go away. She remained still and serene, her face tipped toward him, her green eyes steadily watching him. He felt the beat of wildness in her. Everything about her— the way she stood, the shine of her eyes, the moist line of her upper lip—was an invitation.

Mentally, emotionally, he tried to brace himself against her. His breathing became shallow and uneven.

"You get everything you want, don't you, Irene?" he said at last.

"Most of the time, Bill," she whispered. There was a pause while the suffocating excitement within Horn increased. Then she added very softly: "There's just one thing more."

"What's that?" he asked and was immediately sorry he had been trapped into speaking so quickly.

Her smile was rich and languorous and knowing.

"Do you have to ask that?"

There was no reserve in her, only a strong, compelling eagerness that drew him forward. His arms went around her and he kissed her hard and hungrily.

It was a long kiss, but suddenly in the middle of it Horn found himself thinking of Kay. He felt the warm, fervent response of Irene's lips while the excitement within him slowly waned.

Irene sensed his withdrawal. His arms slackened their pressure around her waist. She drew away, her eyes puzzled and inquiring.

The gunshot came, then, sharp and clear in the night. It woke echoes among the bluffs that stretched beyond the far side of the river. There was a surge of heated air going past them, followed by the slap of a bullet in the timbered side of the packet.

Horn whirled, pushing Irene roughly to the

deck. His Colt slid into his hand and he laid two answering shots among the few bales that still littered the landing.

At a low crouch he ran along the deck to the gangway. His nerves were on edge, waiting for another shot that never came. Boots pounded down the companionway and Dave London appeared.

"What's the shooting about, Bill?" London asked, his own gun jutting from his hand.

"Get down, Dave!" Horn snapped. London dropped to his knees and Horn went on: "Someone took a pot shot at me from the landing. Irene was with me. The bullet might have hit her." He broke off to glance toward the landing. Two of the crewmen who had been left on board to guard the packet came running, but Horn sent them away. "I'm going ashore to have a look," he gritted.

Without a word London rose and followed the *Western Star*'s pilot down the gang-plank. Deep darkness shrouded the landing. Horn proceeded cautiously, gun fisted, keen eyes questing through the shadows.

"Take the south end," he whispered to London.

London slipped away and Horn went on among the barrels of cases. There was no sign of activity along the river.

A shuffling noise off to Horn's right jerked him around.

"That you, Dave?" he queried cautiously.

"Yeah." London ran lightly up to him. "The landing is deserted, Bill. Did you see anyone?"

"No. We're too late. Whoever it was has had all the time in the world to circle back to town and mingle with the crowds." Horn threw a truculent glance toward Yankton. "Let's go back."

They retraced their steps to the *Western Star*. Irene was waiting for them on the freight deck. She hurried up to Horn.

"Bill—did you find anyone?" she asked nervously.

She was trembling. He had to take her hands and hold them firmly, reassuringly until calmness returned to her.

"Come along," he said. "We'll go to my quarters."

He guided Irene to the companionway and with London following them they went up to his spacious cabin on the boat deck. There was a neatly made bunk near the window fronting the deck. On the oblong table in the centre of the room was a big coal-oil lamp. A few marine prints with neat wooden frames hung on the painted walls.

Horn pulled out a chair for Irene. When she was seated he moved around behind her to draw the blind on the window. Then he came back to face her.

"Did you come down to the landing alone?"

The question seemed to surprise her.

"Of course not. Lieutenant Breadon walked me here from town." She watched him a little uncertainly. "We'd been for a ride earlier in the afternoon."

"Did you see anyone else around the landing when you got here?"

A thin glint of anger stirred in Irene's eyes.

"Why this cross-examination?" she demanded hotly. "I'm free to do as I please."

"I don't give a damn what you do," Horn said sharply and saw the shock of his outburst hit her like the slap of a hand. But he continued with equal roughness. "I'm trying to get some idea about who was doing the target practising down there. That bullet didn't miss you by an awful lot."

"Could it be Jayhawkers?"

Horn shook his head impatiently.

"I want to know if you saw anyone around the landing when you came down with Breadon."

"No one."

"Just you and Breadon."

"Yes." Her eyes dropped.

"That's all I wanted to know." He stopped and caught London's speculative glance upon him, but declined to give the other man a clue to the nature of his thoughts. "Whoever it was, is either a damned poor shot or a damned good one."

London looked puzzled.

"What are you driving at, Bill?"

"The bullet was far from spent when it went

85

past," said Horn. "That means the fellow firing that gun was pretty near the boat. Anybody with a reasonable amount of skill should have been able to hit Irene or me. Yet, the shot was uncomfortably close enough to lead me to suspect the man wasn't trying to hit anyone. He meant to miss, but he also meant his shot to come close."

Understanding flooded London's weather-seamed cheeks.

"Someone from the camp?" he queried.

Irene broke in hastily: "But who could it be?"

Toughness moulded the corners of Horn's long mouth.

"I don't know," he said, "but I intend to find out."

Chapter 9

At reveille two mornings later General Macy's three companies of cavalry started to break camp. Sleepy-eyed troopers rolled out of their blankets, struggled into their boots, then strapped on sabres and gunbelts, tilted their garrison hats, with the crossed sabre insignia gleaming above the straight visor, to a jaunty angle on their heads.

All of Yankton turned out to see the expedition off. Women with shawls clasped around their shoulders leaned out of windows. Other younger women lined the streets or waited down near the landing, looking for some fond and familiar face that must be dearly remembered because it might never be seen again.

Bill Horn stared through the windows of the pilothouse and over the thick sheet metal that had been set up as a shield for bullets. Sunlight put an amber sheen on the silt-laden surface of the Missouri. Horn turned to General Macy standing at his side.

"Whenever you say, General."

Macy took a final look at the shore. The landing stages had been drawn in and lashed to the decks. The mooring lines had been freed and deckhands were rolling them up. The general nodded to the pilot.

Horn lifted his hand to Kay Graham who was watching him from the glass-enclosed pilothouse of *The Queen*, then tugged at the whistle cord. A shrill blast of sound echoed up and down the river. He grabbed the engine room signal lever and asked for half-speed reverse.

Immediately the throbbing pistons of the *Western Star*'s engines picked up their beat. Waves of vibration sped through the deck planking. The huge paddle wheel churned up a muddy froth at the stern. Slowly the *Western Star* slid out toward midstream.

Horn swung the packet around in the channel

and headed upstream, the engineer instantly meeting his demand for half-speed ahead. One by one the other packets steamed away from Yankton and pointed their prows toward Fort Union and the wilderness.

The weather held good for the first week as they sped northward past the Niobrara, the White, and the Cheyenne rivers. On clear, moonlit nights they kept going without stopping to make camp. Otherwise, Horn usually selected some wooded island in midchannel or a sheltered cove at which to tie up for the night.

During that first week Horn saw very little of Irene. He spent most of his time in the pilothouse, guiding the *Western Star* through the treacherous, ever-shifting channel of the Missouri. Mile after muddy mile the threat of snags, sand bars, and sawyers had to be met. It was a job that required eternal vigilance.

They were passing the mouth of the muddy, turbulent Cheyenne river when Horn encountered Irene at the foot of the companionway leading to the boat deck. It was the middle of the afternoon and a dry, intense heat filled the land. Irene was dressed in a pale green frock that matched the rich green colouring of her eyes. He smiled his pleasure at seeing her.

"Hello, Irene. Let's take a turn around the deck. I've been cooped up in that pilothouse most of the day."

"Too late, my friend," said a heavy, vibrant voice behind him.

Whatever Irene had been about to say was left unsaid. She and Horn turned together, seeing Breadon who had hurried up behind them. The lieutenant stood stiff and straight, garrison hat tipped jauntily over one ear, his blue uniform moulded to the solid, muscular lines of his body.

"Meaning what?" said Horn, not liking Breadon and deliberately letting his feelings show in his voice.

Breadon's lips moved in a twisted smile.

"Mcaning I've got a prior claim."

The shadow of rising temper showed in Horn's eyes.

"That so, Irene?" he asked.

She blushed, looking from Horn to Breadon and back to Horn.

"I did sort of promise to walk with the lieutenant and—"

"That settles it, then," broke in Horn.

Breadon's grin widened.

"I reckon it does, Horn," he said. "Better go back to your little glass cubbyhole."

Anger poured an immediate and savage heat through the pilot.

"When I need advice from you, Lieutenant, I'll ask for it."

Breadon's right hand knotted and he tried to step around Irene. His blunt chin was thrust forward. Before he could speak, however, Irene had taken Horn by the arm.

"You're not angry, are you, Bill?" she asked. She was coy again and soft, wanting to pull him back because she feared he might be slipping away from her.

"No, Irene," he replied shortly. And even as he said it, he realized how true this was. He felt no anger toward Irene. He was filled with an odd indifference toward her.

The lieutenant was spoiling for trouble. Horn was ready to give it to him. He even took a step toward Breadon when he remembered that the success of Macy's expedition might very well depend on everyone working together. A fight with Breadon would be a bad move. If Breadon had any following among his men, it might alienate the troopers against Horn and his crew.

Accordingly, Horn stopped, gave the officer a hard, level stare, and turned away. He nearly swung back again when Breadon gave him the rough edge of his sly smile—a smile that broadly hinted that Horn had backed down.

The expedition saw its first Indians ten miles beyond the junction of the Cannon Ball and Missouri rivers. Dave London made the discovery. He was on his way to the pilothouse when he happened to glance up at the slate-covered bluffs that hemmed in the river's eastern shore.

Standing motionless on a flat rock were six

Sioux braves. All of them were armed with rifles.

London hurried to Horn with the news. The pilot immediately abandoned the wheel to London and sent one of the deckhands after General Macy. The commander arrived in less than a minute. He joined Horn on the texas. Together they regarded the Indians above them.

As far as they could determine, the Sioux were in full war paint. Though the redmen made no attempt to fire on the packets steaming past their position, Horn knew that their keen dark eyes were probing each boat and estimating the amount of troops and supplies massed on the decks.

"There are your Indians, sir," said Horn. "The first we've seen, but hardly the last."

Macy turned serious eyes upon the pilot.

"I expect you're right about that, Captain." He walked to the rail and peered down at the troopers lined along the promenade. Most of them had grabbed carbines and were staring intently at the Indians. "I left orders with my officers that there was to be no firing from the boats unless we were attacked."

Horn nodded his agreement. "There'll be plenty of fighting where we're going. The Sioux will be ready for us."

Macy rubbed the flat of his palm along his square jaw. The packets were drifting beyond the Indians, but they still maintained their stolid vigil.

"I fully expect that," he acknowledged. "But I'd

like to know what leads you to that conclusion."

There was no hesitation in Horn's answer. His years spent on the Missouri, bucking the wilderness with a steamboat, fighting Indians, trapping, and hunting wild game, had given him a fund of valuable experience from which he now drew.

"We should have been seeing occasional bands of Sioux long before to-day," he stated to Macy. "The fact that we haven't can mean only one thing. The various Sioux tribes have got together. They are probably concentrating their forces farther to the north. I daresay they've been expecting us and when the time is ripe for them they'll strike."

"From what I know about the Sioux," said Macy. "I'd say you've got them pegged correctly. From now on I intend to keep guards posted on every deck. I suggest you warn the other boats to be prepared for trouble at any time.

"I am particularly anxious that the boats carrying the horses stay close. If the Sioux ever succeed in killing a bunch of our cavalry mounts our campaign will be crippled before it can start."

"A good idea, sir," replied Horn. "I also suggest doubling the guard detail when we stop at wood camps."

Later that same afternoon two more Indians were spotted atop a high promontory.

Then for several days they saw nothing. No Indians. No signal fires. Yet the very absence of the Sioux served to heighten the tension of the troops.

Nerves were strung wire-tight. Each man was like a coiled spring. Sentries watched the bluffs until their eyes threatened to pop out of their heads. The very air seemed to vibrate with the growing pressure. It was like a powerful heel grinding them.

And the heel ground more deeply when they halted at a wood camp opposite the Knife River and discovered the Sioux had been there before them. Horn had gone ashore with members of the crew from the *Western Star* and *The Queen*, accompanied by a guard detail under the command of Lieutenant Breadon. Made wary by the absence of the woodcutters who never failed to approach the shore to cheer the arrival of steam boats, the group immediately fanned out into skirmish lines.

Breadon sent his men forward cautiously. They spread out among the trees, watching for signs of Indians in the brush. They saw no Indians, but they did find the woodcutters.

The six men were scattered about in a small clearing, their bodies riddled with bullets and arrows. Abandoned saws and axes lay nearby. Cut logs were stacked in several big piles at the edge of the clearing.

After a few moments a sergeant reported to Breadon that no Sioux were in the vicinity.

All the next day they steamed up the Missouri without seeing any further signs of Indians. And then in the middle of the next afternoon the attack they had all been expecting came with a jarring suddenness. One moment they were slipping past a line of low bluffs that were apparently empty of life. The next moment a horde of yelling Sioux Indians jumped into view and rifle shots began riddling the weather-worn sides of the five steamboats.

Chapter 10

Bill Horn, his tall body bent over the wheel, ventured a quick glance at the bluff which had miraculously filled with Sioux warriors, then rang the engine room for half-speed.

As the packet lost headway in the channel he grabbed the whistle cord and tugged at it four times in quick succession—a pre-arranged signal with the other steamboats carrying the cavalry horses to move up behind the *Western Star* and *The Queen*.

The cliffs seemed to be alive with crawling savages. They would fire a few rounds at the packets, then duck out of sight behind boulders or shallow outcroppings of rock. Horn thrust the carbine to his shoulder, laid his sights on a tall warrior who rose from his hiding place to fire down on the *Western Star.* The gun was lifting to the Indian's shoulder when Horn's carbine roared. The big Sioux warrior dropped his rifle. It clattered on the rocks, skidded over the edge, and dropped to the river. Then the warrior took a few reeling steps and followed his weapon into the muddy current.

There was a shout below Horn, somewhere on the promenade deck. A woman's voice cried in answer. Then feet pounded up the companionway, coming toward Horn. He fired a shot from his carbine and glanced back over his shoulder. Irene's head came level with his eyes, then the rest of her body. She was breathless from running. The white look of fear thinned out her cheeks.

"Irene!" Horn yelled. "You were told to stay in your cabin!"

"I couldn't. I—I was afraid." Her lips trembled and the shadow in her eyes deepened. Hot lead churned wildly over the deck.

"Get down, Irene!" Horn shouted.

She didn't seem to hear him. She kept coming. A Sioux arrow whizzed past her and buried its flint head in the wooden railing beyond. From the companionway came another yell.

"Irene! Where are you?"

It was Lieutenant Breadon. He climbed into

Horn's range of vision as Irene crossed the open area near Horn's position.

"Down, I say!" Horn cried and flung himself at her. His shoulder struck her knees. She teetered backward, fighting to retain her balance. She fell on her back. Horn crawled near. His eyes blazed. "You little fool. Are you trying to get yourself killed?"

She raised startled eyes to him. Her lips drooped in a scarlet smear of terror. He took her roughly by the shoulders, dragged her past the companionway that led to the pilothouse until he reached the narrow passage that ran between the rail and the officers' cabins.

"Now stay there until we're out of this."

He turned his back on her, ran at a low crouch to the companionway. Breadon, his face sweating and full of the dark wash of rage, charged toward him.

"Damn you, Horn!" he growled. "You're rough with your tongue and rough with your hands. Irene is no deckhand—"

"Get down!" Horn shouted. His hand descended on the lieutenant's shoulder with all his strength. Breadon, thrown off balance, dropped to a knee. "For an army man you don't show much sense. Those Sioux up on the bluff will gun you down as quick as the next man."

Breadon's knuckles were dead white as his hand closed swiftly over the stock of his carbine.

He swung it around toward Horn. Horn ignored the menacing barrel, keeping his eyes on the cavalryman's face.

"Keep your hands off Irene," Breadon said finally, his voice thick with wrath. "You've got a lesson in manners coming to you."

"Later," Horn snapped as he threw his carbine to his shoulder and fired at a moving brown shape up on the bluff.

He saw with a growing sense of unease that the channel was narrower at this point. The bluffs on either side of the Missouri were pinching them in. And the Sioux were running along the rocks, keeping pace with the progress of the packets.

Suddenly Horn realized that the *Western Star* was travelling at a reduced rate of speed. The knowledge startled him. A small bubble of worry rose within him. Some odd compulsion drew his glance to the glassed-in pilothouse of *The Queen*.

Kay Graham was up there, leaning over the wheel. With an extended arm she was gesturing toward the open water ahead of the *Western Star.* There was a grim urgency in her usually calm features.

Horn started toward the bow. Above him there was a tinkling crash of glass. He looked up. London had knocked out a portion of a window-pane with a block of wood. He lowered his face to the jagged opening.

"Bill, we're trapped!" he shouted. "Buffalo!"

Horn's apprehension increased. His lips drew together in a taut line. He ran down the passage beside the officers' cabins, temporarily protected from the Sioux attack, until he reached the bow. There he halted, feeling the bubble of worry expand and burst within him. A sick, cold despair held him rooted to the spot.

Just seventy yards ahead of the *Western Star* the granite walls of the canyon flattened out. Beyond, and extending far to the eastward, was a broad, grassy plain. The meadow was like many another swale in Dakota and Montana where huge herds of buffalo grazed, gorging themselves on the juicy grass.

As far as Horn could see the plain was dotted with their moving black shapes. The great shaggy beasts had no doubt been feeding there all day. Now the sudden appearance of the steamboats and the thunder of rifle fire had stampeded the animals into a wild charge across the river.

Snorting and bellowing, they rushed from their feeding ground. Their clumsy bodies left the river bank and plunged into the swift-running current. Ten and twelve abreast they swam toward the other shore, intent on escaping the thunder of guns that spelled danger to them.

A dull, roaring sound filled the air. It penetrated the sound of soldier and Sioux guns. On and on the buffalo came, in a never-ending phalanx. Across the broad plain, over the bank, and into the muddy Missouri. Slipping and sliding on the far bank, they hefted their shaggy bodies out of the water and went rumbling away.

"We'll never get through them!" said Breadon as the *Western Star* drifted to within twenty yards of them and London's signal from the pilothouse stilled the packet's motors.

The yelling Sioux warriors, still hundreds strong, were clambering down the slopes of the bluff, intent on getting close for a more concentrated assault. It occurred to Horn that the Indians had deliberately set up this trap, taking advantage of the buffalo herd's presence in the area. They knew the packets would be stopped by that wall of animals which now choked the Missouri's channel. While the boats waited for the buffalo to go by or tried to escape downstream, the Indians would be able to exact a fearful toll of lives.

"Bill! Bill! What will we do?" gasped Irene.

Horn turned. He had not heard Breadon come up behind him. Now he was surprised to see Irene. She leaned against him, an agony of fear shaking her slender frame. She watched the churning tide of bodies in the Missouri with a sort of horrible fascination. Even now stray buffalo drifted past the packet, their heavy bodies slapping against the sides.

Horn pushed Irene away.

"There's a chance," he said. "I'll have to take it."

"What are you going to do?" Breadon asked.

Horn ignored the question. He went to the rail, leaned over.

"Murphy! Agnew!" he shouted at the top of his lungs.

There was a brief wait. Then a beefy-faced roustabout with close-cropped black hair appeared below. He glanced inquiringly at Horn.

"Yeah, Captain?"

"Murphy," said Horn with a savage urgency riding his voice. "Remember where you and Agnew stowed those cases of dynamite and caps?" When the deckhand nodded, Horn went on: "Well, I want one of those cases right now—with fuses and percussion caps. Take as many men as you need. But get them up here fast—and see that you're covered by a good volley from the troops. Tell Macy."

Murphy grinned and ducked away. Then Breadon's rough hand fell on Horn's arm, jerking him around.

"Are you figuring on blasting the Sioux out of those rocks?" the lieutenant demanded. His high forehead was creased by a deep frown.

There was a temporary lull in the Indians' firing, for they were scrambling down from the higher promontories and preparing to take up new positions at the edge of the plain.

Watching them, Horn let out a startled and gusty breath.

100

"What is it?" Irene whispered.

"Breadon!" Horn snapped the word out. "Look over there. White men are with those Sioux!"

Breadon studied the rocky slopes. Paint-daubed Sioux warriors flitted from boulder to boulder, now and then hidden by occasional clumps of brush. The bare bronze skin of the Indian braves glowed redly in the fading glow of the westering sun. There was abrupt flash of brighter colour— the glimpse of a red checkered shirt, then a yellow neckerchief. A white bearded face peered out of the rocks. Another smooth-skinned face poked around a brush clump, then vanished.

"By God, you're right!" breathed Breadon. He lifted his rifle, sighted a long time toward the shore before squeezing the trigger. A mild curse escaped from his lips. "Missed the white-faced skunk."

"Jayhawkers probably," said Horn, his face like a grey mask.

Irene looked at him. She immediately thought of Jack Wade and knew that Horn was thinking of him, too. She started to say something to break the tension, but the fierce destructiveness that bannered out of his eyes at this moment made her hold her tongue.

A heavy fusillade from the decks of the *Western Star* and *The Queen* warned Horn that the roustabouts must be making their run with the dynamite. All over the packet carbines were firing. A cloud of grey gunsmoke drifted lazily past the prow of the boat. The Indians on the rocks hastily sought cover.

"Answering your question about the dynamite," Horn said to Breadon. "I intend to use it on the buffalo."

Breadon stared at him incredulously.

"You don't mean that."

Horn gestured to the shore. The Sioux were forting up in a deep cut-bank arroyo. Others took refuge behind convenient boulders that dotted the edge of the plain where scores of buffalo were galloping frenziedly toward the river.

"The Sioux have good protection," Horn pointed out. "We'd have to drift too close to shore to be able to use the explosives effectively. It would involve a double risk on our part. The nearer we get to the Sioux the greater their chance of picking off the troops and horses. Also, we might run aground on a sand bar. I don't need to remind you what that would mean."

There was a shout behind them. Horn and Breadon swung around. Murphy and another husky deckhand appeared at the stern. They carried a small wooden case between them. Closely following them was another roustabout with a smaller case. The last man had a crude bandage around his head and blood was dripping down his left arm. Horn spoke to him.

"The redskins wing you?"

"Yeah," was the curt reply. "Nothing to bother about."

Murphy said, "Where do you want the stuff?"

"Right here."

"Need any help with it?"

"Just break open the cases," said Horn. "You can leave the rest to me."

The two cases were placed carefully down on the deck. Murphy produced a finely tapered bar of iron. He thrust the pointed end under the lid and pried upward. Nails screeched as they were forced through the wood. Then the top of the case came off, exposing rows of dynamite sticks. Murphy bent to the other case. It contained fuses and percussion caps.

"All right, Murphy," said Horn. "That's all and thanks."

The beefy-faced roustabout nodded. But he lingered a few minutes with his two companions to watch Horn. The pilot yelled for Dave London. The mate left the wheel and came to the smashed portion of glass in the pilothouse.

"Dave!" There was a ringing quality to Horn's voice. "Quarter speed ahead. I want to get close to those critters."

"Right!" said London and hurried back to the wheel.

A bell clanged far down in the engine room. Black smoke plumed from the packet's twin chimneys. The vibration of sliding pistons pounded through the thick deck planking. Slowly the *Western Star* cut through the Missouri's turbulent flow. The snorting and bellowing of fear-crazed buffalo knifed sharply through the air. The thick mass of their passage across the river was only a few yards away from the packet's prow.

Horn bent to the wooden case and picked up several dynamite sticks. He took up some short lengths of fuse, then fitted fuses and percussion caps to the dynamite. He kept one length of fuse free, lighting it with a sulphur match and touching the flame to the other fuses.

He rocked his arm back and hurled three sticks of dynamite into the midst of the buffalo. Fuses sputtering and flaming, they arched through space, disappearing in the mass of shoving swimming bodies.

There was a dull *bloom*. A ragged rent was torn in that living black wall. Fountains of water, darkened by segments of raw flesh and bone, spurted up from the river's surface. Yet the gap remained there for only a brief interval. Almost immediately, other buffalo swarmed into the free area, driven there by the pressure of the animals behind them.

The prow of the *Western Star* was at the edge of the herd now. Horn signalled to London to reverse his engines. The packet slid backward a trifle while Horn readied more sticks of dynamite. Again and again he hurled the sputtering loads of explosive into the mountainous barrier of churning flesh that blocked the channel. Again and again huge holes were torn in the barrier. Dead buffalo were trampled by other animals or went drifting downstream past the packets.

At the edge of the rocks the Sioux, understanding what their white rivals were endeavouring to do, increased the fury of their attack. Guns blasted back and forth. Now and then the scream of a wounded man was carried to Horn's ears or the frightened whinny of a horse. But more than anything else, he heard the booming explosion of the dynamite, the ragged bawling of the frightened buffalo.

Chapter 11

Horn was starting on the final row of dynamite sticks before he noticed a break in the movement of the herd. The last charge, widening a gap previously made in that wall of bodies, suddenly halted the rush of buffalo toward the river.

A dozen shaggy-headed bulls, frightened by this new peril erupting in their midst, began to mill and circle along the bank. Behind them other bulls and cows and calves pressed forward. One or two of the advance bulls were forced over the bank into the Missouri. But gradually, the rest of the animals fell into an aimless circling as they sought a new avenue of escape.

With the frenzied rout of buffalo temporarily halted, Horn yelled to London up in the pilot-house.

"Send her through, Dave!" He waved his arm toward the bloody, debris-littered water ahead of the packet. "Full speed."

London's answer was to tug on the whistle cord to notify the other packets to get up steam. The Sioux back along the edges of the plain began a renewed yelling as the *Western Star* glided forward.

Bullets and arrows hissed through space, splintering into the packet's sides. Macy's soldiers returned the Indians' fire shot for shot while the revolving paddle wheels carried the boat out of range.

Dead buffalo floated on all sides. The *Western Star*, gaining speed, thrust the obstructions aside. Kay Graham at the wheel of *The Queen* delayed her advance until the other packets had run the gauntlet.

It was the massed ranks of soldiers on *The Queen*, firing as rapidly as they could, who covered the flight of the other boats. And by the time *The Queen* had steamed through the clutter of dead buffalo carcasses the entire expedition was out of range of the Sioux guns.

Horn, still gripping a stick of dynamite in his fist, watched the Indians and the buffalo slowly recede from view with a grim smile of relief on his powder-grimed features. He bent down, put the dynamite back in the case.

When he straightened Irene rushed into his arms. She let her weight sink against him.

"Bill! Bill!" she sighed. "We got through—thanks to you." She looked up at him, her hands stroking his arms. "Darling, you were wonderful."

Horn stood stiffly before her. His body was rigid. His arms remained at his sides.

"Well, aren't you even going to kiss me?" Irene whispered.

If she remembered that Lieutenant Breadon was directly behind her, she gave no sign. She looked at Horn with an insistent feminine attention, her eyes warm and deliberately provocative. She was, therefore, a little startled when he pushed her away.

"No, Irene. I'm not going to kiss you."

"But, darling, you know—"

She let her voice trail off and brought her soft body once more against him. He grimaced. There it was—that "darling" again. He stepped away from her.

"You're a little late, Irene," he said. Some of the roughness of his feelings got into his speech. "You haven't had any time for me during the past few weeks. Now suddenly you're back again.

107

I'm tired of waiting for you to make up your mind about the man you want."

"Bill! Please!"

He went on unheedingly. "I've come to the conclusion that you aren't capable of an honest emotion. First you had me. Then came Jack Wade. Something happened there. Then you came back. After that it was Breadon. Now it's me again. And to-morrow it'll be someone else. It'll always be that way with you. Maybe you can't help it. But I know this—I'm through."

Breadon stepped past Irene to confront Horn.

"I agree with the last thing you said. You're through." The red flag of rage coloured his olive-skinned face. "I said before you were too rough with your talk. That still goes."

Horn was expecting the blow that followed Breadon's statement, yet it came so swiftly that he was unable to roll sufficiently with the punch. Breadon's knuckles grazed his temple with enough force to knock him back against one of the officers' cabins.

He bounded away from the wall and ran into another savage blow that cut his upper lip. The raw, salty taste of blood filled his mouth. He grinned, liking the taste and liking the thought of this fight.

Breadon swung again—wildly. Horn came in under the blow and struck with a long, rapier-like left that hit the lieutenant high on the right cheekbone. He took a jab to the face, rolled with another wild left, then charged again. And now he tallied with deadly precision. A left under the heart, a left to the head, and a savage right cross to the chin that spun Breadon around and sent him sprawling to the deck.

The lieutenant was slow to rise. When he did get up he staggered as if the motion of the boat was too much for his equilibrium. Head down, he moved toward Horn. Then something in Horn's gaze lifted the cavalryman out of his crouch. He was already whirling around as General Macy, accompanied by Lieutenant Lowell of A company and Lyle Ferriss, the medical officer, hurried along the deck.

Macy gave Horn and Breadon a quizzical glance, then managed a weary smile.

"Using that dynamite to blast a path through those buffalo was quick thinking, Captain," he said to Horn. "In plain words, you saved our bacon."

Horn acknowledged the compliment with a tight smile of his own.

"It was touch and go for a while."

"Another fifteen minutes of pounding from the Indians could have been very serious," Macy informed him.

Horn's face sobered instantly.

"Did you lose many men?" he asked.

"Four dead and seven wounded."

"We were lucky, then," said Irene.

Macy frowned. Horn said flatly:

"Losing even one man on an expedition like this is unlucky. We've just had a sample of what to expect from the Sioux. I've a feeling we're going to need every available man before we're finished."

"I agree," snapped Macy. "And there are still the other boats. We don't know what their losses are."

Captain Ferriss clicked his white teeth together and rubbed a finger up and down his high-bridged nose.

"If the general pleases, I'd like to make some arrangements to take care of the wounded."

Macy turned to Horn. "That's what I came to see you about. As soon as you consider it safe enough to stop I'd like you to do so in order that the wounded can be transferred here from the other packets."

"With that buffalo herd between the Sioux and ourselves I don't believe we'll be running any great risk," Horn answered. He waved to London up in the pilothouse. When London pulled down one of the sliding panes of glass Horn called out: "Watch for a cove where we can tie up for a while, Dave."

"Right, Bill," said London and slid the glass back into place.

Macy drew Horn's attention by making another request.

"Can I make use of your officers' cabins for the wounded?"

"You sure can," responded Horn. "That goes for my own quarters, too. And if Captain Ferriss needs any nursing help Kay Graham will probably be glad to lend a hand. Tug Willison can handle *The Queen* in her absence."

"We'll need her," chimed in Ferriss. He turned to Irene. "And you, too, Miss Nostrum. I understand from the general you did a little nursing in a Union hospital in St. Louis."

"Put her to work, Lyle," said Macy. "I didn't want Irene along on this expedition. No place for a woman, anyway. She talked me into it because she said she might be useful just for this purpose."

Irene didn't appear too pleased with the general's suggestion. She nodded rather nervously. Her eyes were large and round in her white face. No one noticed her distress except Horn. He said nothing, but a slow suspicion was born in his mind.

The *Western Star*'s whistle blew shrill and the packet began to veer toward shore. A thick grove of trees grew within a hundred yards of the river bank. But between the trees and the river was a level meadow sloping down to a gravelly bank. Fortunately the water was deep enough to enable the packets to slip in close without running aground.

One by one the packets ran down their gang-planks. Deckhands raced ashore with great strands of rope to make their ties around the boles of the nearest trees. General Macy and his officers marched off the *Western Star* and were immediately met by the lieutenant commanding the forces on *The Queen* and by the sergeants who had been in charge of the guard details on the other steamboats.

Horn came ashore also and started toward *The Queen*. Kay Graham, serene and beautiful in a full, flowing blue dress, anticipated his visit and met him at the foot of *The Queen*'s gang-plank. She gave him a bright smile—a smile that expressed her real pleasure at seeing him.

"Bill, that was very nice work back at the buffalo crossing," she said.

She extended her hand to him and, though he took her fingers in both his hands, she pretended not to notice it. She had spoken without coyness. It was a simple expression of admiration. Nothing more than that. Horn thought of that and was again reminded of the direct and straightforward way this woman said and did things. There was no artifice, no play-acting, in her manner.

He felt at home with her—which was a feeling he had never enjoyed with any other woman. This was no time for an expression of his sentiments toward her. He knew that. But he also knew that she had the power to colour and influence all his thinking. Alongside Kay, Irene was pale by comparison—a shallow, selfish, and flighty girl with no solid substance to her.

There was something earthy and strong and wild about Kay. She radiated vitality and energy. Yet, with all that, she was completely feminine, with all of a woman's gifts and charms to give to a man—if she were ever moved to surrender herself.

Now Horn smiled at her, aware of the hunger in his eyes and not caring if she noticed it.

"Kay, we might just have time for a walk. What do you say?"

She regarded him through eyes that were veiled and curious.

"If you like, Bill," she murmured quietly.

"Good," said Bill. He took her right arm, then added, "But before we go, I wonder if you wouldn't go back on board the *Western Star* with me. I've something in my cabin I want to show you."

There was a vague hint of excitement in his voice and again she gave him a veiled, curious stare. She was searching for the meaning behind his words and was puzzled by his odd eagerness.

"All right," she said at last.

He led her back to the landing stage. They boarded the *Western Star*, crossed the freight deck to the companionway, and started toward the texas.

They were climbing past the promenade deck when London called to Horn from the stern.

"Later, Dave," said Horn and pushed Kay ahead of him. He saw London frown and gesture above him, but he could not understand what London was driving at so he continued on.

They reached the texas, started along the port side where the officers' cabins were situated. They came to Horn's stateroom. Kay glanced sidewise at him, seeing his excitement increase, seeing a strange shine in his eyes.

Horn put his hand on the knob of the door. Suddenly it turned under his fingers. The door was flung inward. Irene came out. She stopped, a deep flush covering her cheeks. Beside him, Horn heard a slight gasp from Kay. Then—only then— did he see the filmy lace nightgown that was draped over Irene's left arm.

"I—I'm sorry," she said falteringly, looking confused. "I—I left this back there . . ." She gestured vaguely behind her. Her long eyelashes fluttered briefly in Kay's direction. "I—I didn't mean to have you see . . ." Again she broke off. Then, before Horn could stop her, she darted away down the deck.

Horn stood rooted to the deck. Shock and bewilderment deadened his senses. It was the sound of Kay turning beside him and moving away that brought him back to glaring reality.

"Wait, Kay. Wait!"

She paused a few feet away, one hand white tightly gripping the rail.

"Is that what you wanted to show me?" she asked, with a withering calmness.

"No, Kay. It's crazy. Irene had no right—"

"Don't bother to explain," Kay interrupted coldly. "I understand how those things are." She started to walk away.

Horn ran after her, caught her at the top of the companionway.

"But that's just it. You don't understand," he said. "I don't know how or why Irene—"

The shrivelling contempt in her eyes stopped him.

"Let go of my arm, please," she said.

He dropped his hand, then suddenly reached for her again. He caught her by the shoulders.

"Listen, Kay. You've got to believe me. I was going to—"

For just the briefest of intervals Kay's control slipped. A dark shadow deepened her eyes and her full, rich mouth trembled. Then she mastered her feelings again and her eyes sparkled with rage.

She twisted away from Horn. She hit him savagely with the palm of her hand. He fell back, his fingers involuntarily stroking his cheek.

She said with sharp finality. "I'm not interested in anything else you have to say."

She turned away, then, and went down the companionway. And this time Horn didn't stop her. He watched her go and it was like watching sunshine fade out of the sky. The light was gone and suddenly only darkness was left.

He hadn't yet had time for anger. Misery and shock were too deeply engraved in his mind. He retraced his steps toward his state-room. He went inside. The room was quiet and severely masculine—as it had always been. Yet there lingered a faint scent of perfume, the musky, provocative perfume that Irene always used.

He came out on deck again. The fresh air seemed to clear his head. Anger came then. He saw it all. A little too late.

Irene was a clever little actress. The scene outside his cabin had been carefully planned. That was obvious now. Because Irene had lost him and because she couldn't bear to let another woman possess him, she had resorted to this devilish trick to discredit him in Kay's eyes.

The memory of that pink, frilly garment hanging over Irene's arm and the memory of the brief, hurt look he had seen on Kay's face, sent him charging along the deck.

He didn't even see Dave London when the latter tried to stop him near the gang-plank. He brushed past London, rushed down to the shore. He had noticed Irene walking down beyond the last supply packet. He saw her look back, then quicken her pace when she saw him set out to follow her.

In two minutes he had overtaken her. She was about to enter a narrow path that led off into an aisle of trees when he caught her by the right elbow and twisted her around.

"Please, Bill," she murmured. There was fear in her voice and the red flag of shame in her face.

"That was a mighty low trick, Irene," he said and the depth of his anger made him sink his fingers into her arm. "If you were a man . . ."

She came close to him.

"You know why I—I did it, Bill."

He looked down at her tear-filled eyes, at the moist curve of her mouth and suddenly his anger evaporated and he felt a disquieting sense of pity for her.

"Yes, I know," he said. "But it's no go and it can never be again."

He wheeled abruptly away from her, then, and strode back down the line of steamboats. He saw now that Macy and his aides were gathered at the foot of the *Western Star*'s landing stage. He saw Kay come up to the group, speak briefly with the commander, then go aboard his packet.

Macy broke off his discussion with his company officers when Horn joined them.

"I'm starting to move the wounded now," Macy explained.

The general gestured to the packet behind *The Queen*. Two troopers could be seen descending the gang-plank, bearing a stretcher between them. Reaching the shore, the soldiers stepped carefully toward the *Western Star.*

Another group walked down the gang-plank with a stretcher. But the man they were carrying was covered with a sheet. Horn's lips set grimly. He knew he was seeing the first of the dead men to come off the boats.

"How many men did we lose, General?" he asked.

"Twelve dead and ten wounded," replied Macy. His dark eyes reflected the deep remorse he felt for the men he had had to sacrifice to get through safely.

The pilot of one of the other steamboats spoke up.

"Those figures include two troopers who were dragged over-board when some of the horses broke loose on deck."

"Also two of Kay's deckhands," added Tug Willison, a round, barrel-chested man who served as Kay's mate and assistant pilot. The marks of many a rough-and-tumble barroom brawl were on his weather-seamed cheeks, yet he was a bluff, good-natured man.

Another stretcher went by with a dead soldier. Macy watched the litter bearers march toward the end of the clearing. Then he turned to Lieutenant Tom Lowell.

"Tom, take a detail of twenty men over to the edge of the trees and start them digging."

Lowell said, "Yes, sir." He saluted and marched off.

Three minutes later he passed with twenty troopers each of whom carried a spade over his shoulder. The grim work of burying the dead was ready to begin.

A few more wounded men were carried aboard the *Western Star.* Then Lieutenant Husking of E company reported to Macy.

"The wounded are all aboard, sir," he informed the general. "Captain Ferriss has requested the assistance of Miss Nostrum. Miss Graham is already aboard, but—"

"I thought Irene was with him," interrupted Macy. He whirled around, saw Irene walking slowly along the bank. "Irene, come here."

The girl turned around and retraced her steps with obvious reluctance. She avoided Horn's glance.

"What are you doing out here when Captain Ferriss needs help with bandages and instruments?" Macy demanded.

"But Dale—" She broke off and a rush of blood coloured her fair cheeks.

"What is it?"

"I—I can't go up there."

"You can't?" Macy looked startled.

"The blood—the moans—and—" Irene's voice shook and she dropped her eyes from the general's face.

"You should be used to that by this time after working in an army hospital," Macy said. Then his eyes narrowed with suspicion and he added: "Wait. Tell me. Did you really work in a hospital?"

Irene's answer was a miserable whisper of sound. "No, Dale."

A brittle silence fell upon the men gathered at the foot of the *Western Star*'s gang-plank. Muscles knotted in Macy's cheeks. He was so angry he couldn't find anything to say. Horn, too, was silent as he regarded her with a mixture of pity and contempt.

"Damn it, Irene," said Macy finally, "I only let you go along because I figured you might be useful on just such an occasion as this. Why were you so set on going?"

Irene looked helpless and lost. She floundered about, seeking an explanation that would satisfy Macy. She glanced quickly at Horn, then looked away. Macy saw that brief glance and a faint light of understanding came into his eyes. Then his face hardened.

"Ferriss has orderlies to help him," he said, fighting for coolness. "But there are some things a woman can do better than a man. One of them is nursing. Kay Graham is up there now. And that's where you're going—whether you like it or not."

She hesitated, rubbing her hands together. In spite of his anger and contempt, Horn felt sorry for her.

"Go ahead, Irene," Macy said.

"All right, Dale."

She lowered her head and walked past him, going up the gang-plank.

An hour later Macy's three companies of cavalry stood at attention in the clearing, garrison caps in their hands while the bodies of their dead companions and the two deckhands were lowered into shallow graves. The trumpeters stood idly by, trumpets in hand. With the Sioux still dangerously near, Macy did not wish to risk calling undue attention to their activities. And so taps were dispensed with.

Macy's voice droned swiftly through the brief burial service. Then he closed the book, nodded to the troopers waiting with their spades. Hard clods of earth began to fall into the graves. The troops saluted, replaced their garrison caps on their heads, and were dismissed.

Within another thirty minutes the graves were filled and the burial detail returned to the *Western Star.*

Darkness was falling rapidly, but an early moon promised a good night for travel so the five steamboats backed out into the channel and continued their journey toward Fort Union.

Chapter 12

The landing was filled with soldiers, trappers, half breeds, and a scattering of Indians when Dale Macy's floating army rounded the last bend and came in view of Fort Union opposite the mouth of the Yellowstone.

A loud cheer went up and the wind carried the sound to the blue-clad cavalrymen who crowded against the forward rails of the *Western Star*. Somewhere within the stockade a cannon boomed. The echo of the salute had barely died away when a volley of rifle fire from the packet's decks sounded in reply.

A tall flagstaff thrust its slender shape high above the stout bastions. The flag whipped jauntily in the stiff, morning breeze. The sight of the flag, of the huge stockade with its weather-worn pickets, the two-story house of the bourgeois, and the line of shouting soldiers tugged strongly at Bill Horn's feelings.

The polished wheel spun under his fingers as he heeled the packet past a slightly submerged snag. He signalled the engine room for half speed, felt the answering quiver in the deck flooring as the pounding pistons reduced the rhythm of their beat. He pulled the whistle cord and all down the line behind him the other packet pilots added the shrill din of their whistles to the mounting surge of sound.

Paddle wheels revolving at quarter speed, the *Western Star* slid up to the landing. Even before the deckhands could leap ashore trappers and soldiers came together in groups to grasp the mooring lines. The gang-plank was run out and troopers began to march ashore. They broke ranks quickly to mingle with friends among Companies G and H.

Behind the *Western Star* Kay Graham was deftly berthing *The Queen.* The three remaining steam-boats puffed up to the landing. Gang-planks slammed into place. Troopers, working under a red-faced sergeant, began to lead the cavalry mounts ashore.

A bugle shrilled assembly call as Horn emerged from the glassed-in pilothouse. From the landing and out along the prairie that led to the trading post soldiers melted out of chattering, laughing groups and swiftly formed orderly ranks.

Captain Al Haggard, commanding Companies G and H, rode a sleek-flanked black horse through the cavalry ranks, then dismounted at the edge of the landing. Handing the reins to an orderly, he stepped forward to meet General Macy. He lifted his hand to his forage cap in a crisp salute which the general returned. Then they shook hands.

"I'm glad to see you, Al," said Macy.

Haggard, a young serious-looking man with dark brown hair and eyes to match, smiled briefly.

"Thank you, sir," he said. "We've been expecting you for the past week. You had no trouble?"

"A little," said Macy. "A band of Sioux attacked us a few miles below the Little Missouri. We almost didn't get through when a herd of buffalo picked that time to cross the river ahead of us."

"How many men did we lose, sir?"

"Twelve dead and ten wounded."

Haggard frowned, but said nothing.

"You're thinking we could use every one of those men," said Macy.

Haggard nodded. "We could, sir. The Sioux are in strong force in this area. We've run across several bands of them."

"Any forays against the fort?"

"No, sir. That'll come, though, unless they're beaten this summer."

"That's what we're here for, Al."

The full heat of summer was on the land. Burning rays from a white sun had seared the green prairie grass to a dull reddish-brown. The wind, whipping across the plain, was hot and dry.

"Let's move along to the fort," said Macy, but he paused when Horn came up to him.

The general introduced him to Captain Haggard.

124

Then, leaving instructions with Lieutenant Tom Lowell to see that Kay and Irene were provided with suitable living quarters, Macy directed Horn to follow him.

Haggard led the way to the big trading post which had been built in 1829 by that great trapper and buffalo hunter, Kenneth McKenzie. For a distance of more than two hundred feet hand-hewn pickets stretched along the prairie to form the redoubtable wall of the stockade.

They entered the wide gates and crossed the spacious courtyard with bastions twenty-four feet square and two stories high erected at opposite corners for defence. The bastions were constructed entirely of rough field stones and each had a pyramidal roof.

At the far end of the courtyard stood the house of the bourgeois with two stone chimneys, glass windows, and a broad gallery. The rest of the courtyard was occupied by barracks, warehouses, stables, fur press, ice house, and blacksmith shop.

The American Fur Company, which operated Fort Union, also ran other trading posts along the huge watershed of the upper Missouri. Horn, who had often been within the fort, was again struck by the decline in the post's activities. At one time it had been recognized as the greatest fur trading post in the wilderness. It was here that most of the Indian tribes of the Northwest had come to barter their furs for food and rifles and colourful trinkets.

It was here that the great trappers and voyageurs had trekked at the end of their long forays to the Musselshell, Three Forks, Great Falls, and the rugged valleys of the Rocky Mountain chain.

In the last year or two, however, trade had fallen away sharply. Many of the trappers had made Fort Benton their base of operations. Others, drawn by the news of gold strikes around Bannock, had followed the wandering Missouri to its very end, ultimately swinging down the Jefferson River, one of the three streams that came together at Three Forks to form the Big Muddy, till they reached the edge of the Continental Divide.

The war, too, and the subsequent increase in Indian disturbances had had its effect upon life at Fort Union. Whereas the post was normally filled with Indians come to trade their furs, their crude lodges being thrown up on the prairie outside the stockade walls, now only a few friendly Crows and half breeds were to be seen lingering in front of the store where all trading was done. With the Sioux gathering in strength throughout the territory it was becoming increasingly perilous for the Crows to make their long trips to the fort.

Captain Haggard took Macy and Horn directly to the two-storied house generally occupied by the factor of the post. Because the factor was away they were made welcome by his assistant, a middle-aged, dark-bearded man.

Introductions were made on the broad gallery, then the dark-bearded man invited the newcomers inside. Just before he stepped through the door, Horn noticed several foot soldiers crossing the far corner of the courtyard from a low, squat barracks building.

The big front room with its huge stone fireplace never failed to surprise Horn. McKenzie had furnished the house lavishly when constructing the fort and some of the long-vanished splendour was visible in the faded, decorative paper that still draped the walls and in the thick, but worn carpet that covered the puncheon floor.

After a brief talk with the factor's assistant Macy was told that the two ladies as well as his officer staff and the steamboat captains could be accommodated in the house.

Macy immediately dispatched an orderly to summon Lieutenants Lowell, Breadon, and Husking to the house for a preliminary discussion of field plans for the forthcoming offensive against Wild Horse and his Sioux warriors.

As soon as the officers arrived chairs were drawn up around the great table that many times had sagged beneath the weight of lusty dinners of beaver tails, elk steaks, buffalo hump ribs, wild partridge, and pheasant. Haggard produced a crude map of the area with the prominent branches and creeks and mountains clearly marked.

General Macy began the discussion by questioning Captain Haggard about the disposition of the Sioux bands around Fort Union.

"Where did you last run into some of the red warriors?" he asked.

"About twenty miles east of the Little Missouri," said Haggard.

"Any fighting?"

"None. Just spotted a band of them. About one hundred. They were young bucks and travelling light. We couldn't come up to them."

"When was that?"

"Five days ago," said Haggard.

"Any sign of other Indians in the area?"

"Yes, sir. Plenty. We cut the trail of another band of about three hundred coming from the north. And on the way back to the fort we ran across tracks of another band evidently in from Beaver Creek."

Macy digested that information, a deep frown furrowing his brow. He tapped a finger on the map, lifted his glance to Haggard's face.

"There seems to be a general movement of the Sioux to the south and east. Have you any idea where they might be concentrating?"

"Possibly around Killdeer Mountain. Rough country there."

Horn signalled to the general that he wished to say something and Macy nodded.

"Captain," said Horn, "did you see any signs of white men running with the Sioux?"

128

Haggard gave him a surprised look. "No. Why do you ask?"

"Because there were white men with the band of Sioux that attacked us below the Little Missouri."

"Renegades," said Haggard with a curl of his lips.

Horn nodded. "Yeah. Jayhawkers and deserters from Jeff Davis' rebel army."

Haggard's face showed his disbelief. "They're a long way from home. What would they be doing up here?"

"We ran into a bunch of them at Pittsburg Landing. From what we heard at Sioux City and Yankton some of the Jayhawkers have moved pretty far north. In fact, I'd bet they've had something to do with stirring up Wild Horse's band."

Haggard stared at Macy, as if waiting for the general to confirm Horn's statement.

"I reckon what Horn says is true," said Macy. "Don't forget that every Union soldier diverted up north here eases the pressure just that much on Lee in Virginia and Beauregard in the West."

"I doubt if Wade is worrying about Lee or Beauregard anymore," said Horn. Bitterness and anger pulled at his words.

"Wade?" queried Haggard.

"The man we believe to be leading the renegades who have joined up with the Sioux. Captain Horn has every reason to remember him."

Haggard's keen glance shuttled to Horn, but the latter shrugged and answered curtly.

"That's a story I'll tell you sometime."

Macy bent down to study the map again and the others drew nearer to watch his finger trace a line southeastward from Fort Union across the Little Missouri to Killdeer Mountain.

"As I see it," he said after a moment of silent concentration, "there are two courses open to us. We can sit here in the stockade and wait for Wild Horse to gather his warrior bands together and make his foray against Fort Union. Or we can take the offensive—carry the fight to him. Go after him right away, force him into action before he can consolidate too strongly." He stopped and looked around at his officers. "Can I have your opinions, gentlemen?"

Lieutenant Breadon said without hesitation, "Go after him now, sir. That's the only way."

"I agree with that notion," said Lieutenant Lowell.

When Macy glanced toward Husking and Haggard they, too, signified that they were in complete agreement with Breadon's sentiments.

"Good," said Macy. "That was my own feeling." He stared down at the map, his mind already sifting and sorting the possible moves he might make to carry out the campaign. "We'll need at least two days to drill, to exercise the horses, and prepare supplies for the pack train. I'll want to leave Fort Union at dawn three days from now."

"It can be done," said Haggard.

Lieutenant Lowell leaned forward to catch Haggard's attention. "Didn't I see some infantry soldiers around the stockade?"

"You did. There are two companies under Major John Thomson. They're on their way back to Fort Pierre. They're stopping over a few weeks."

"That's a break for us," said Breadon. He studiedly avoided Horn's gaze, keeping his glance upon Macy. "It means we can take all the cavalry on this campaign and leave the infantry to guard the fort."

Macy said, "Yes, I'd thought of that. We're apt to need every man during the next week or two." His eyes narrowed in speculation and the others waited for him to go on. "I figure on a two-week trip—or at the most sixteen days. If we don't contact the Sioux in eight or nine days we'll turn back."

Haggard said, "It'll be dangerous to extend ourselves beyond that, sir. Those redskins can travel around for weeks and live on a few strips of dried jerky and a swallow of water. We can't do that with all the gear we tote around. And it's going to be damned hot crossing the badlands around the Little Missouri."

"How about civilian scouts?" Macy asked abruptly. "Have you been using anybody?"

"Nobody around that's available," said Haggard.

131

Macy protested at once. "But I saw several trappers and hunters down at the landing."

"They're passing through. None of them hanker to mix in with the Sioux this trip. That's one of the things that's kept us back on our scout details. We couldn't risk going too far. The water holes are few and far between."

"I'm at your service, General," said Horn to Macy.

"What do you know about scout work?" snapped Breadon.

Macy waved his hand at the young officer. "Never mind, Jim." He swung around toward Horn. "I was thinking of using the *Western Star.*"

"You mean to try navigating up the Yellowstone?" said Horn.

"Yes. Do you think it can be done?"

"A boat with a shallow draught might do it."

"The *Western Star*?"

Horn considered a moment, then said, "*The Queen* would be better. Draws less water. That'll be mighty important—especially in midsummer."

"What about Kay Graham?"

"She can take a steamboat any place I could. She's your bet, General. And, as for the scouting, I'd like to go along. I've hunted and trapped in that country around the Little Missouri many times."

Macy's weather-burned face showed a faint pleasure. "Looks like we need you, Captain."

He left the table and took a nervous turn up and down the room. His officers watched him, not saying anything. Then he came back to them, looked at the map once more, and appeared to reach a decision.

"Here's the plan, gentlemen. Miss Graham will pilot her packet up the Yellowstone as far as Glendive—if the water is deep enough—" He broke off to look at Horn.

"She can use spars if it's necessary," Horn said.

"All right. Glendive Creek it is, then. She will carry reserve supplies for us. We will leave Fort Union and travel south and east, trying to pick up the trail of the Sioux. If we do cut any sign we follow it and try to force the Indians into a fight. If we don't run into them we'll draw back to *The Queen* for fresh supplies and move out again, swinging south toward the Heart and the Grand rivers."

Chapter 13

The first grey light of dawn was cracking through the heavy bank of clouds that lay along the eastern horizon when the shrill call of a trumpet, blowing reveille, echoed across the courtyard of Fort Union.

Swiftly the sleeping camp came to full, vigorous

life. The sound of grumbling voices drifted from the barracks where heavy-eyed troopers rolled out of their bunks and mechanically reached for their boots.

Ten minutes later the trumpet blew again, summoning the troops for roll call. The foghorn voices of company sergeants reeled off the names of their enlisted men. "Hallett, Busby, Grayson . . ." And in crisp, staccato tones came the reply of each man. "Here . . . Yes, sir . . . Present."

By the time roll call was completed and the sergeants had reported to their company lieutenants and received orders to dismiss, the smell of coffee and bacon and fresh bread filled the morning air.

There was a crisp tang to the breeze. But in two hours, when the sun had pushed above the rim of clouds, summer's heat would drain all the moisture out of the air and the wind whipping in from the flats would beat against the fort and all of these men like the blast from an ore-smelting furnace.

Men drifted across the parade to the mess hall and, in a little while, tramped out again. Down at the landing black smoke began to puff from *The Queen*'s twin smokestacks. The shambling figures of several deckhands wrestled crates and barrels up the slanting gang-plank to the freight deck.

A dozen troopers assigned to water detail

appeared from the stables, leading the cavalry mounts down to the river. Another detail burdened with strings of canteens slung around their necks ambled over to the well alongside the post store. Then, as the horses drifted back from the Missouri the soldiers in the pack detail set to work loading the pack animals. Extra rations of food, huge canvas sacks of water, entrenching tools, extra rounds of ammunition were swiftly lashed down and covered with tarpaulin.

The column was ready to travel and the few trappers and Crow Indians and the clerks of the American Fur Company were gathered to watch them off when General Macy emerged from the factor's house with his staff of officers.

Macy lingered on the gallery a moment to watch the massed rows of blue cavalrymen, carbines slung across the pommels of their saddles, heads lifted, and eyes looking straight ahead. A fine bunch of men, Macy thought—and a powerful fighting force. And then came the nagging question: But were they enough to beat back the Sioux?

That was a question only time could answer. Actually, they were riding into the unknown. For weeks now Wild Horse had been collecting his scattered bands of painted warriors. And only the Sioux knew how many Indians were massed against the threatened invasion of the white soldiers.

Macy shrugged his mood of depression aside

and tramped down the steps. A few yards away from the gallery Kay Graham was waiting. Although Horn had been watching for her, Macy's broad back had hidden her from his view. Therefore, when he did see her he could not hide the shocked start of pleasure that immediately sprang into his face.

He heard Lieutenant Breadon a step behind him call out, "Irene," but the name did not register with him. He moved away from the gallery, absorbed and overwhelmed by Kay's serene beauty—the new blue dress that draped her softly moulded figure, the rosy colour in her cheeks, the clear light in her eyes. He caught her glance and smiled, not sure how the gesture would be received. She nodded curtly and her eyes gave him no warmth, no invitation to approach.

Then another voice called his name and Irene was standing before him. She let her hand rest timidly on his arm.

"Good-bye, Bill," she whispered. Her eyes were hot and anxious. She flinched before his stern, unsmiling glance. "Don't be so hard, Bill." Suddenly she pulled his head down, reached his mouth with her lips. She added quickly, "Take care of yourself," and turned away.

Horn watched her hurrying figure for a brief second, then looked over at Kay. Her features were cool and remote. Lieutenant Lowell came over to her and she gave him her hand and added a warm smile. The young, good-looking officer had removed his campaign hat and his face mirrored a ruddy pleasure as he murmured good-bye to Kay.

Lieutenant Breadon crossed the compound, his eyes eagerly searching the loosely knit groups of people. He saw Horn and looked away. Then he saw Irene a few yards away—saw her turn back toward Horn. Breadon, his features suddenly intent and ugly, glared at Horn and intercepted Irene before she could reach the pilot.

Horn ignored Breadon's jealous glance and walked over to Kay who was already moving toward the stockade gates. She paused when he came up to her.

"Aren't you going to say good-bye, Kay?" he asked.

She stood rigidly still. There was a sober look about her. A flicker of her strong will showed in the sombre, unemotional way she stood before him. It reminded him once more of the wall of reserve she had flung up between them since the unfortunate scene outside his cabin.

Since that afternoon Kay had studiously avoided him. She had permitted no shadow of intimacy between them. When business brought them together she spoke to him. But never did she allow anything personal to creep into her talk. She was a stranger—aloof and unreachable.

Now her long, full lips softened just enough to

permit a little smile. But she refused to meet his eyes.

She said, "Good-bye," and gave him her hand. She withdrew it when he tried to retain it. "Good luck," she added quietly.

"Thanks," he said.

He looked for some sign of warmth in her voice, some hint of a break in her reserve. There was nothing. He stepped close. His big hands took her shoulders and pulled her in. He felt her immediate resistance, saw the dark danger signals rise in her eyes, and he murmured desperately, "Kay, is there nothing I can do or say to show you—"

Macy's voice, ringing across the compound, came between them.

"Time to go!"

Horn let his hands drop. He saw how stiffly she stood. He murmured, "Good-bye, Kay," and walked away without looking back.

An orderly was holding his horse. He took the reins and swung into the saddle. Breadon and Lowell mounted nearby. Horn followed Macy to the head of the column. And as he rode there was a tightness in all his muscles, a miserable, burned-out feeling in his heart.

A cheer rose from the company of infantry that remained behind. Then the column wheeled and trotted through the open gates of the stockade.

Down to the landing they marched. Both the

Western Star and *The Queen* had steam up. The column split up, half moving toward Horn's packet, the remainder toward Kay's boat. Each packet made two round trips ferrying the troops to the south side of the Missouri. Then with both steamboat whistles blowing the column rode away across the flats.

They travelled steadily for three days before they cut any Indian sign. The Little Missouri was thirty miles behind them and they were pushing across a shallow creek that formed one of the headwater streams which later joined to form the Knife River when the break came.

Horn, exploring the rugged, rolling country a mile ahead of the main column, suddenly turned in his saddle and lifted his hand. Then he sat loosely in the saddle and waited for the command to catch up to him.

General Macy, flanked by Lieutenants Lowell and Breadon, spurred up alongside Horn who now dismounted and pointed to a broad set of tracks which emerged out of the north, cut directly across their line of march, and continued on in a southeasterly direction.

"There's your Sioux," said Horn.

Macy twisted in his saddle, gave a low-voiced command to Al Haggard a few yards behind him. Haggard saluted, turned, and ordered the troops to dismount and take their ease. At once the men tumbled out of their saddles and gathered in small groups as they squatted on the ground.

Macy, Lowell, Breadon, and Haggard crowded around the pony tracks that showed in the dry earth.

"Those prints aren't much more than a day old," said Macy. "What do you think?"

Horn nodded his head in agreement.

"How many in the party?" the general asked.

"Three hundred, maybe more," said Horn. "Just bucks in war paint, I'd guess. They're travelling light. No women or children."

The tracks were widely spread and the distance between the individual hoof prints of each horse indicated that the Indians had been proceeding at a rapid gait.

Haggard rose from a close scrutiny of the tracks and said with an eager, almost boyish grin, "Looks like they're in a hurry to join some of their friends farther south."

Macy stood up, looked away in the direction the Sioux trail wandered over a bald ridge.

"Maybe we can give them a little surprise," he said. "Let's be on the move."

Horn came up to him. "Better put a couple of extra men out on the flanks from now on."

"I will," said the general. "And I'll send Haggard with you. Two pairs of eyes are better than one."

"All right." Horn turned to Haggard. "Here we go."

He moved back to his rangy black gelding and lifted himself easily into the saddle. Haggard mounted, joined him at once, and together they rode away to the southeast.

At an order from Breadon the rest of the command returned to their saddles. Canteens clanked at the end of their metal chains and saddle leather creaked under the burning rays of the sun as, two by two, the cavalrymen swung into the trail taken by the Sioux.

Macy singled out four troopers, sent two of them off to the right to join the flankers already patrolling the far ridges, and dispatched the other pair to the left to join the flankers there.

In that manner the column moved on through the rest of that day with only a brief pause near noon for lunch. They followed the up-and-down contours of the land, now climbing some steep, bare grade, then winding through the narrow corridor of some canyon, and again crossing wide areas of flat, arid terrain, the dry white particles of earth resembling the twinkling grains of desert sand.

For brief periods of time the troopers out on the flanks would be visible as they rode along the crest of some distant ridge. Then they would vanish as the trail dropped behind an intervening fold of land.

Meanwhile, Horn and Haggard pushed steadily on. They drove their mounts to the top of each new rocky eminence. There they would pause to study the ground stretching away in front of them before plunging forward once more.

Although the command travelled at a fast pace all afternoon there was no way of determining if they had picked up any ground on the Sioux. The Indians' trail appeared no fresher than it had looked earlier that morning. Finally they camped for the night beside another small tributary of the Knife River.

After fires were kindled and the horses had been watered and staked out to graze, guards were dispatched into the outer darkness to patrol all the approaches to the camp. The smell of frying bacon and coffee began to fill the air and the men collected in friendly groups to eat and talk and smoke.

When supper was finished most of the men curled up in their blankets and fell asleep. They had ridden long and hard and in the days to come there would be no surcease from the hot, tortuous hours in the saddle.

But in front of Macy's tent there was still activity. At the general's invitation, Horn and the rest of the staff officers had had supper with him. Now, with Macy puffing at his pipe and striding nervously up and down, they waited for him to speak.

"We didn't pick up any ground to-day," he said suddenly to Horn.

"When Indians have a mind to travel no cavalry regiment can keep up with them," Horn told Macy.

"Do you figure they know we're camped on their trail?"

"I'm sure of it."

"How? We haven't seen an Indian all day."

Horn shrugged. "When an Indian doesn't want to be seen, you just don't see him. But I'll bet a month's revenue from the *Western Star* that they not only know we're trailing them but also that Kay Graham and her packet are waiting for us at Glendive Creek."

Lieutenant Breadon offered an immediate objection.

"Hell, the way you talk you'd think those redskins have second sight."

"Sometimes I think they have," Horn answered, unmoved.

Macy's thoughtful glance lifted to Horn's face.

"What do you suggest?"

"Stay on their trail for another day or two and then see—though I've an idea we won't catch them." Horn was about to elaborate the point, but something in the keen, watchful glances of Macy's officers decided him against it.

But Macy, shrewd observer of men, pinned him down.

"You've got an idea. Let's have it."

"Call it just a hunch," said Horn. "And I could

be wrong. Let's wait and see. If I'm right there'll be only one thing left for us to do."

For a moment Horn thought the cavalry commander was going to demand a full explanation, but then he abruptly changed the subject and began talking of routine plans for the next day's march.

An hour after dawn the column took up the Indians' trail again. By midmorning the flanks of the horses were lathered with sweat and the broken contours of the land hung limp and lifeless in summer's blazing heat. The creak of saddle leather and the jungle of bit chains was more and more punctuated by the clink of metal canteens as the cavalrymen took long drinks of water to slake their thirst.

They crossed the Heart River shortly after noon, the water running very shallow, even for that time of the year. At three o'clock they reached a dry stream bed where Horn had hoped they could fill the canteens and water bags. Usually this small creek only dried up very late in the summer, but now the sandy, caked earth between the banks gave mute evidence that the stream had given out at least a week before.

It wasn't until nightfall that they came upon a small tributary of the Heart that enabled them to replenish their water supplies. By that time the command was worn out. Horses and men had been severely taxed. The heat had sapped their energy, leaving them dried-up husks.

There was no talking after the supper fires had been put out. Instead, the men sprawled out where they had eaten and fell into an exhausted slumber. Thereafter, the camp was utterly still except for the muted thud of footsteps on the outskirts of the picket lines where sentries paced back and forth.

The next day was a repetition of what had gone before. More sun, more heat, endless trailing with dried-up streams and water-holes appearing like evil omens of the future. The Indians' path of travel began to swing back toward the west late in the afternoon. It wasn't a full swing—rather a half swing so that they found themselves travelling southwest instead of straight south as they had done the day before.

For two hours the trail held steadily to that southwesterly direction and Lieutenant Haggard, riding alongside of Horn two miles in front of the command, saw the troubled frown that ridged the pilot's forehead—a frown that grew deeper all the time until it altered the whole cast of his face.

"Something wrong?" Haggard demanded, his words coming a little thickly because of the dryness in his throat and mouth.

"I don't like it," said Horn and drew up suddenly.

He dismounted, went over to study the tracks

the Indians had made in passing, then returned to his horse.

"Signal the command to come up," said Horn. "We'll wait here."

"Hell, man!" said Haggard. "What did you see? What are you worked up about?"

Horn swallowed convulsively and looked longingly at the canteen strapped to his saddle. Dust and grime caked his face and his lips felt stiff and swollen. He glanced at the welter of hoof prints in the earth and then stared up at the brassy ball of the sun and a premonition of trouble shook his shoulders.

Haggard's insistent stare drew his attention again.

"Later, Lieutenant," he said. "Talking isn't easy now and I've an idea it may be important to go easy on the water."

He spoke calmly enough but it was his very restraint that filled Haggard with a strange and compelling sensation of unease. All at once he was impressed by the vast unfriendliness of this rugged land. It was a land without mercy—the boiling sun in the cloudless sky, the barren earth, the empty stream beds with the deep ugly cracks in the baked ground they had seen that day, all bore witness to the animosity of Nature, an enemy that could be more terrifying than a thousand lodges of Sioux.

The point of the column came toiling up the

146

grade. The men sat slack and loose in their saddles, their faces showing the downward pull of weariness, their eyes jaded and empty. Macy signalled to Lieutenant Lowell to give the troopers their ease, then cantered forward to join Horn and Haggard.

"Are we getting closer, Captain?" Macy asked eagerly.

Horn shook his head and gestured to the pony tracks in the earth still stretching away to the southwest.

"The Sioux are still a day's ride ahead of us, General. We're not going to catch them—at least, not by following this trail."

Macy took a bandanna and wiped dirt and sweat from his brow. His tongue came out to lick his dry, chapped lips.

"What do you mean?" he asked finally.

"Two nights ago when you asked me I wasn't quite sure just what the Sioux were up to. Now I think I know." Horn, too, had to stop to run his tongue across his lips before he could go on. "Two hours ago the trail swung to the southwest and I'm willing to bet that in another day, or perhaps two days, the trail will swing straight west."

He stopped, letting Macy consider the implications of that conjecture. At first the general appeared to be puzzled. Then his eyes widened and his voice took on an added sharpness.

"You mean the Sioux are leading us back toward the Little Missouri?"

"Back toward the Little Missouri and maybe even the Yellowstone," said Horn. "From all the signs I'd say this was a big band of Sioux we're following, yet they're deliberately avoiding a fight. I think I know why. They're expecting to strengthen their forces somewhere ahead. Meanwhile, this is the middle of summer when these badlands are plain hell and the waterholes dry up everywhere.

"It would be a damned clever move on Wild Horse's part to let us wear ourselves out chasing them while our supplies run out—and then hit us from in front when we're about ready to drop. We've been travelling at a hard pace for three days. Take a look at the horses. They show it. And so do the men."

Horn paused while Macy and the other officers involuntarily glanced at the jaded cavalry horses and at the troopers sprawled out on the ground to snatch these few precious moments of rest.

"We can expect trouble from here on in," Horn resumed, "and probably most of it will come from natural causes. For one thing, we'll have to ration our water. This whole country is drying up fast. There are one or two small feeder streams of the Cannonball River and the Little Missouri between us and Glendive Creek. That's all and it isn't much."

General Macy shook his head stubbornly.

"I don't doubt you're right about that, but we've got to keep after those Sioux. That's our job—why we were sent up here."

"You'll meet them soon enough," said Horn. "They won't let us get out of this country without a fight. But right now my advice is to abandon the Sioux trail and head fast for the Yellowstone. My guess is that the Sioux will try to cut in ahead of us before we get there. We've already travelled too far on our rations and the feed for the horses has been mighty sparse. Take it from me, it won't get better. Two more days of steady going in this heat, trying to overhaul the Sioux, will kill half the horses."

Macy was silent after Horn had finished. He glanced toward the west where the sun was fast sinking in the cloudless sky. The land—barren and rocky and smothered in heat—stretched on and on in endless brown folds and hills.

"You don't paint a very pretty picture, Bill," Lieutenant Haggard murmured with a wry grin that the dryness in his mouth somehow turned into a macabre grimace.

"What you've seen of this country hasn't been pretty," Horn said bluntly.

"We're after Sioux, Captain Horn," cut in Breadon with a calculated and biting preciseness. "If we leave their trail now they'll figure we're afraid to come to grips with them. Maybe that's your trouble. You're scared."

The last sentence was uttered softly, but the words carried an unmistakable sting. Haggard stiffened and looked around at Breadon who was watching Horn and thinly smiling.

Temper made its brief, muddy stir in Horn's eyes. Then he faced Breadon squarely and answered with a savage directness.

"Sure I'm scared. Only a damned fool wouldn't be. And it's not only of Wild Horse and his Sioux bucks. Whether we meet them or not, we've got a fight on our hands—a fight to get back across this sun-baked hell to the Yellowstone without losing half the command." He suddenly ignored Breadon and turned to Macy. "We're low on food and there won't be any wild game to shoot this time of year. We're going to have to get along on what we have and pray that our horses hold out."

The matter was argued back and forth for another twenty minutes but eventually General Macy decided to follow Horn's course of action. It was a decision made only with the greatest of reluctance. But, whatever else might be said about Macy, he was a commander who would not needlessly risk the life of a man in his regiment. And he fully realized that to continue to trail the Indians might take the column farther and farther away from their base on the Yellowstone and leave them still more at the mercy of this fierce and merciless land.

At Horn's suggestion a voluntary system of water rationing was instituted when they camped that night. The troopers were warned that they could expect to find no fresh water until they reached one of the small tributaries of the Cannonball late the next afternoon. Therefore, they were advised to limit their evening ration to three swallows.

It was a bitterly unpleasant order to carry out, for the food they ate refused to go down past their parched throats and the few swallows of water hoarded for the end of the meal only served to increase their craving. More than one trooper surreptitiously drained his canteen, hoping that Macy might dole out extra rations from the canvas water bags reserved for the horses.

In fact, one of the company sergeants, moved by the entreaties of some of the enlisted men, visited the commander in headquarters tent shortly after mess, requesting such extra rations.

Horn was there, together with Lieutenants Breadon, Haggard, and Lowell. Macy hesitated an instant while he ran his sun-browned fingers up and down the cords of his neck. When he spoke his voice was hoarse and strained and more blunt than he intended it to be.

"You can inform the men of all companies that there will be no extra rations given out—unless we fail to find water by the end of to-morrow's march."

Breadon's face showed a grey, straining misery. He said in a thick, almost desperate tone, "The men are suffering. This heat has been plain hell. A little water now would lift their spirits."

Macy frowned. Involuntarily he glanced toward Horn. The riverboat pilot shook his head. Breadon saw the gesture and flushed in anger.

Horn said quickly, "I don't think we can risk it, sir."

"What do you mean, risk it?" Breadon demanded. "The men are thirsty. Hell, I'm thirsty." He dug his fingers inside his shirt collar, swallowed with an effort. "What's more important—the horses or the men?"

"The horses, of course," snapped Horn. He saw the shocked rage narrow Breadon's eyes. "That should be elemental to a cavalryman. We're several days from the Yellowstone. Without horses we'll never get through and they need water just as much as we do."

Breadon started to protest, but Macy silenced him with a wave of his hand.

"Captain Horn is right, Lieutenant. You're miserable now—just like all of us. But we can't risk pulling down the endurance of the horses any more than we have already." Macy directed his next words at the sergeant. "You might also let it be known that I am placing a special guard over those water bags. Any trooper caught trying to secure water from them will be court-martialled when we return to Fort Union. That's all."

The sergeant saluted, spun on his heel, and tramped away. An uneasy silence fell upon the group around the general. Beyond, where troopers lay upon the ground, many heads turned in their direction. They caught the low murmur of conversation. But there was no laughter, no exchange of light banter, no telling of bawdy jokes.

This was a quiet camp, a weary camp—a camp turned morose and bitter and unfriendly by exhaustion and thirst—but most of all, by the dreary uncertainty of what lay ahead.

General Macy broke the silence finally.

"Gentlemen, I mean to retire. I suggest you all do the same. If you sleep you can't think about how thirsty you are. Good night."

The officers snapped to attention. If their salutes were a little slow, a little slipshod in execution, there was a reason for it. They moved away, Lowell and Breadon nodding curtly to each other before Lowell went off to join Haggard.

Unavoidably Horn found himself walking beside Breadon. The big lieutenant's muscular shoulders brushed roughly against the pilot. When Horn turned he caught the full wickedness of the cavalry officer's stare.

"Are you satisfied, Horn?" he asked.

"About what?"

They stopped, of one accord, facing each other,

the old antagonism whirling savagely between them.

"You know what," said Breadon. "The water. If you'd kept your mouth shut Macy might have relented and tapped those water bags."

"I suppose you finished your canteen."

"Yeah. And I'm still burning up with thirst." Breadon leaned close. "You look all right. Maybe you've got an extra canteen."

Horn felt a spasm travel along the muscles of his arms and back. His fists knotted. But when he spoke there was an iron control in his words.

"Better try sleeping, Lieutenant. This is no time for petty arguments."

Breadon cursed. "Someday, Horn—" His words trailed off thickly as Horn met his glance with an unwavering directness. Suddenly he swung around and walked off in the swiftly gathering gloom.

Chapter 14

Despite the weariness that had crept deep into his bones Horn couldn't sleep. He had saved the few swallows of water from his canteen until full darkness had dropped over the land. Then he had let the warm, brackish liquid trickle down his throat, recapped the canteen tightly, and settled down on the ground with his head resting on his saddle.

But he hadn't been able to sleep. He'd kept thinking of the days of riding that stretched ahead. For the first time the full weight of his responsibility in leading the command safely back to Yellowstone settled upon him. He knew the shortest way to travel; he knew just about where waterholes would be found. But he didn't know how many of them would be dried up now.

It was going to be a long, hard pull. Probably Macy and Haggard and the other officers did not yet realize the stark hazards of their position. And always in the background of his thoughts lurked the ugly red spectre of Wild Horse and his Sioux. The Indians could live for days without water, existing on nothing but a few strips of dried meat. The sun and the heat would not take its toll of the redmen as it would of their white pursuers and Horn found himself dismally wondering how long Wild Horse would permit them to travel before he struck.

That Wild Horse would attack he never doubted. The Sioux had led the command on a semi-circular chase—a chase that could easily be turned into a boomerang with the pursued becoming the pursuers. And because he was so certain of the attack, Horn had insisted on taking the shortest route back to the Yellowstone to conserve what little strength they had left to meet the coming test.

He sat up, stared about the camp. Here and there a trooper turned in uneasy slumber. A few hundred yards away the milling shapes of the horses on picket could be seen. A sentry, rifle over his shoulder, tramped past headquarters tent and passed out of sight.

Horn got stiffly to his feet and walked toward the outer sentry lines. The agony of thirst was returning. Those few meagre swallows of water had done nothing to ease the scorching dryness inside him. His throat felt thick. His lips were rough and cracked.

A sentry on the picket line challenged him, then warned him back within the confines of camp. Horn retreated a short distance, then came on again after the sentry had moved along his beat.

There was a haze of dust above the horse corral. It hung like a grey dust cloud against the velvet backdrop of the night sky. A short distance in front of the horses, and separated from them by a rock wall, were the tarp-covered mounds of food —and the canvas water bags.

From behind a huge clump of chaparral Horn saw a man's shape steal softly forward. The man paced toward the special guard whose attention had been attracted by the restless whinnying of the horses.

The sentry was unaware of the man creeping up behind him. To Horn, watching this scene, there was something oddly familiar about that stalking figure. He, too, padded forward.

He was fast, but not quite fast enough. He saw the stalker move right behind the sentry. He saw the guard start to turn in alarm. Then the stalker's right arm lifted and came down with something long and dark at the end of it. The sentry sagged and toppled backward. The man behind caught his limp body and eased it to the ground. Then he moved at a crouch toward the canvas water bags. Horn's low command stopped him before he had gone half-a-dozen paces.

"That's far enough, Lieutenant!"

Breadon spun round in the semi-darkness. His right hand slid instinctively toward his holstered gun.

"You're a fool if you draw that pistol," Horn said, advancing slowly toward him, arms hanging at his sides.

Breadon's wide shoulders stirred restlessly under his blue tunic. Passion put a fine edge on his words.

"Damn you, Horn, some day you're going to get a belly full of lead busting into other people's business."

"This happens to be army business," Horn reminded him. "Or did you forget?" He paused beside the fallen sentry, dropped to one knee to examine the soldier, then rose again.

"How is he?" Breadon asked with quick concern.

"Just knocked out. He'll be all right in ten or fifteen minutes." Horn waited until the lieutenant came up to him. Then he added softly: "You're one helluva man to be an officer. You could be broken back to the ranks for this."

Breadon's eyes were ugly. "Go ahead, and report me to Macy. It ought to give you a lot of pleasure."

"You're wrong about that, my friend. I'm just sorry to see an officer who's a sneak. Macy's going to need every man in the next few days and the men in your troop are going to need a lot of confidence. They'll be looking to get it from you. Don't let them down, Lieutenant."

Breadon stood there, frozen and motionless, unable to assimilate this unexpected reprieve. What he had done could have meant the end of his cavalry career. Now this sudden escape left him quaking, his whole body bathed in a cold sweat.

At last it occurred to him that Horn was waiting for him to go and that the longer he waited the more imminent became the chance of their being seen by one of the other guards. He turned, then, and moved quietly away, going at a half crouch and sticking to the protection of the thorny brush wherever possible.

• • •

From the moment the command broke camp the next morning to ride out under the broiling-hot sun life became an endless cycle of torment to the mounted men. The sky was pale blue and as cloudless as it had been the day before. The barren land lay seared and brown and empty.

Thirst nagged at them until it seemed that their windpipes would clamp shut. No one talked because it required too much effort. The wind, when it came drifting down from the rock-strewn ridges, was torrid and stifling.

To save the horses as much as possible General Macy arranged for fifteen-minute rest stops every hour. Horn went a step farther by dismounting at the foot of each grade and leading his horse to the top. Haggard soon followed suit, as did the riders patrolling the flanks.

They reached the small tributary of the Cannonball late in the afternoon and there they found water. At that, it was barely enough for their needs. Normally a strong freshet rising in the hills, the stream had dwindled to a shallow trickle.

It was that way day after day with both men and horses being steadily drained of their strength. Grass for the horses became scarcer as they went on. The animals grew gaunt; their coats turned ragged and dusty and their heavy bones began to prod their thinning flesh.

One day they travelled from sunrise to sunset

without water. And then in the waning hours of dusk they came to a small spring in a hollow formed by two shelving rocks. The troopers became so intent on reaching the Yellowstone that they no longer gave any thought to the Sioux. They were concerned only with the more immediate problems of thirst and heat and the never ending weariness.

But up to that point Horn never forgot the Sioux. Although he hadn't seen any Indian sign for days he was positive that the Sioux knew exactly where they were. Soon—whenever the wily chief was ready—the Indians would attack. And from the jaded appearance of the command as it wound through a narrow defile behind him, Horn hazarded a dismal guess that they would not have long to wait.

They crossed the Little Missouri and, after a fourteen-hour march, came to Beaver Creek and forded that, too. Macy decided to call a halt beside the stream to give the column a half day of rest. But nothing he did then or later could have helped them avoid the disaster that befell them two days later.

From Beaver Creek they marched all of one afternoon and most of the next day without finding additional water. By that time all the canteens were empty and the extra canvas bags had also been drained. Macy called a conference of his officers. During the meeting Horn informed

Macy that, as well as he could remember, there was one more waterhole between them and the Yellowstone—at a point twenty miles from Glendive.

"How big is that waterhole?" Macy asked wearily.

"A good size."

"Big enough to have water in it after this drought?"

Horn frowned and replied slowly, "I think so."

"How long will it take us to get there?"

Horn glanced up at the sun, then let his eyes shift to the bulky outlines of a few ridges shimmering in the heat waves far to the west.

"If we keep going, we should hit that waterhole around sundown."

Macy scrubbed his cheek with the palm of his hand. There was a burned-out weariness in him and in the men sprawled loosely about him. They were near the end of their tether. None of them could take much more.

He said huskily, "We'll try to make it," and turned back to his horse.

Lieutenant Lowell signalled to the other officers. They, in turn, gave the order to mount. The troopers got wearily to their feet. Their blue tunics were coated with grey dust. The same dust was bedded deeply in the wrinkles of their skin. It seeped into their throats, adding to the misery of their thirst.

Horn and Lieutenant Haggard swung out to the head of the column, moving forward, as usual to reconnoitre the advance line of march.

On and on the column moved, alone in that friendless, heat-scorched land. No one talked. The men rode slackly in their saddles, heads tipped down, eyes half closed to avoid the sun's fierce glare.

They travelled all during that long afternoon. Then, near sundown Horn spotted a tangle of willows a mile ahead. That handful of trees was the only green thing in a land turned brown and grey by heat and sun and wind. Horn felt his horse pick up its gait. Its head went up, the ears moved forward, and it whinnied. Haggard's mount immediately answered.

Horn pulled the horse in, lifted his hand high in the air, and waved the command swiftly forward.

In ten minutes the advance units, formed by Lieutenant Lowell's company, came up. Behind them, in close order, rode the rest of the column. General Macy disregarded the jaded condition of his mount and spurred the animal past the advance units. He said just one word to Horn.

"Water?"

Horn nodded and gestured to the willows. Macy followed the direction of his pointing arm. His face lit up. Suddenly his horse started to fidget. There was a commotion at the rear as the pack horses, too, scented the water, and started away at a trot.

"Forward," shouted Macy hoarsely and the column moved on.

Men and horse perked up magically now at the prospect of water to drink. The troopers straightened in their saddles and the jangling sound of empty canteens bumping against bits of metal on the saddle gear was no longer unpleasant to hear.

The stand of willows rapidly loomed nearer. The command closed up now, the swing riders coming in from the far flanks. Then, when they were within a few thousand yards of the water-hole there was a shout from the rear, followed by the rataplan of hoofs.

Three of the pack horses had broken loose from the string and were galloping past the line of march, the thirst-crazed animals intent upon reaching the waterhole. Several of the troopers swept out of the column to head them off, but two of the pack animals got through.

They clattered down the last slope, skidding to a halt at the edge of the waterhole. A little puff of dust rose beneath their braced hoofs. Then their heads dipped down and they greedily began sucking up water. They drank steadily for perhaps a minute. Then their heads lifted and twisted around to regard the rest of the command coming on at a smart pace.

It was Haggard who first noticed that one of the animals had retreated from the pool and was staggering drunkenly.

"Waterlogged," he said to Horn.

The river pilot watched the horse, saw its companion tremble, sink to one knee, and then struggle to rise again.

"Maybe," he said. "And maybe not."

He kicked his horse forward. There was a shout behind them and several troopers made a rush toward the waterhole. But they couldn't overhaul Horn. Horn got to the edge of the willows, jumped from the saddle, and started toward one of the pack animals just as the creature collapsed and rolled over on its side.

Horn saw the swelling mound of its belly, the distended and bloodshot eyes already rolling in the head. The second pack horse looked sick, too. Horn whirled around as several of the troopers dismounted and started for the pool.

"Hold it!" he shouted. "Don't drink any of that water."

"Why not?" called back one of the troopers.

His companion laughed and dropped to his knees. He was bending his head to drink at the pool's edge—heedless of his own breach of discipline in leaving the column without permission—when Horn's charging body flung him aside.

They rolled over and over in the dust, scuffling

for a moment while the trooper's hoarse cursing drummed in Horn's ear. Horn got up, dragging the soldier with him.

"Shut up!" he growled. "This pool has been poisoned."

He let the trooper go, saw the command sweep around him, pushing him close to the pool's edge. General Macy crowded forward, his startled glance shuttling from the stricken pack horses to Bill Horn and back again. Then he glanced toward the water and a slow horror filled his eyes, turning bleak and hopeless even as he asked:

"What's the matter?"

Horn said flatly, "The pool has been poisoned."

He saw the shock of his words hit the troopers in the column. He saw the men wilt. He saw the hope die in their eyes. And in some he saw the awful desperation—the terrible, driving thirst—that could impel them to drink that water regardless of consequences.

"You're sure those pack horses aren't just waterlogged?" Macy asked, still grasping at straws.

"I'm sure," said Horn. He walked over to the pack animals. Their bellies were terribly swollen now. Their eyes rolled until Horn could see the red-veined whites. The animals were in agony. Their legs thrashed the ground and their breathing was hoarse and irregular.

Horn walked on around the side of the pool, bending down here and there to examine the ground under the willows. He came back, his face white and rigid.

"Indians?" Macy asked, his voice sounding hollow and beaten.

Horn nodded. "Fresh sign, too. Not more than ten hours old. They've cut around in front of us as I expected they would do. This, I reckon, was Wild Horse's trump card." Hard knots of muscle stood out along his jaw line as he added: "And he sure played it to win."

"What happens now?" demanded Breadon, pushing forward.

Horn let him have it without pulling any punches.

"We can stick it out here or make a run for Glendive. Either way we're going to see some Sioux Indians. Wild Horse could have brought on a fight any time within the last week. My guess is that he's been waiting for the right time. That time is here!"

Chapter 15

It was two o'clock in the afternoon when Kay Graham gave the signal to draw up *The Queen*'s gang-plank and swung the big stern-wheeler away from the landing at Fort Union. A faint shout rose from the soldiers, trappers, and the few Crow Indians who had come down from the stockade to see the boat off. Kay answered the cheer with a blast from *The Queen*'s whistle.

Immediately after ferrying Macy's five companies of cavalry across the Missouri, Kay had devoted her energies to supervising the final loading operations. At noon a half company of infantry, under the command of Captain Blaze Sumner, had marched aboard. The troops had been assigned to serve as a special escort for the journey up the Yellowstone. They would be needed to guard *The Queen*'s crew during wood-cutting operations and to protect the steamer from Indian attacks during the long vigil at Glendive which lay deep in the heart of Sioux territory.

Smoke puffing from its twin funnels, the great wooden paddles churning up a muddy foam, *The Queen* crossed the Missouri and angled into the narrower channel of the Yellowstone.

At once Kay had an inkling of what lay in store for her during the upward trip. The boat had hardly traversed four miles when she noted how low the river was. Driftwood was piled along the steep banks, showing the depth of the stream during the early summer freshets when the mountains of the upper Yellowstone had poured tons of water from melting snows into the raging river.

But now the water was very shallow, whirling

and foaming over barely submerged sand bars. As a precaution Kay stationed a deckhand in the bow to take continual soundings with a yawl. The man would yell out the depth of the water and the cry would be passed along to Kay in the pilothouse.

For an hour the boat proceeded in that fashion, the soundings of the man in the bow helping Kay to manœuvre the packet through the channel. Then, rounding a bend, they came to a huge sand bar. The long ridge of soil extended from shore to shore, its yellow surface looming a scant foot below the river's surface.

Kay rang the engine room to reverse the engines. The paddle wheels slithered to a stop and *The Queen* began slowly drifting with the current. Then Kay opened one of the pilothouse windows and called down to Tug Willison to have the spars made ready.

The spars were huge wooden beams which were driven into the river bottom on either side of the boat. Kay watched her crew set to work. First they lowered the posts into the mud, tilting them slightly toward the bow. Then tackle blocks were brought up and rigged on top of the spars. Strong cables were run through the blocks, one end of each cable being fastened to the gunwale and the other end given a turn around the capstan.

Willison signalled Kay when everything was ready. She, in turn, passed the word to the engine room. Slowly the paddle wheels began to revolve, automatically setting the capstan into motion. The combined operation served to lift the boat and push it forward. Then the spars were reset farther ahead and the entire process was repeated over and over until *The Queen* at last reached deep water again.

It was slow, tedious work and it put a strain on everyone. Accordingly, after getting through three such shallow areas in the river Kay handed the wheel over to brawny Tug Willison, the first mate.

"At the rate we're travelling," Kay said, "it will take us a week to reach Glendive Creek."

Willison shrugged, not bothered by any need for hurry. "We've got plenty of time to get there before Macy's cavalry returns." He stopped and an odd smile slid across his face. "Better go down to your cabin, Kay. There's a surprise waitin' for you."

Kay had her hand on the door of the pilothouse when she whirled around and asked: "What is it?"

"Go and see," said Willison mysteriously and shifted his attention back to the Yellowstone.

Kay went out the door, descended the companionway to the texas, and walked rapidly along the deck to her cabin. She flung the door open, pushed inside, then blinked her eyes in the sudden gloom of the interior. She blinked her eyes again when Irene Nostrum rose from a chair beside the crude desk and put down the log book she had been reading.

"What are you doing here?" Kay said sharply.

"You ought to be able to answer that yourself," said Irene with a smile that was half amused and half fearful.

The two girls stood there facing each other with hostility hardening their eyes. A chill came into the room and the strain and annoyance Kay felt poured out of her in a long, ragged sigh.

"Your orders were to remain at Fort Union," she said.

Irene's smile remained, turning more arrogant now.

"Sure. But this trip sounded more interesting."

Kay flushed angrily. "You little fool. Don't you realize we're heading right into the heart of the Sioux country and this little trip up the Yellowstone is apt to be more dangerous than the entire journey up the Missouri?"

"If it's dangerous for me, it's dangerous for you," said Irene.

"Yes, but this is my job."

"Ah, the great heroine!" Irene laughed. It was a brittle sound in the stillness of the cabin and somehow ugly. There was a pinched look about her fine-drawn cheeks. "But I'm here. There's nothing you can do about it."

Kay frowned, and the thrust of her dominant will came out in her soft, deliberate question.

"You think not, Irene?"

The hollows in Irene's cheeks became more distinct, but she spoke with a careless bluster.

"Maybe you're thinking of putting me ashore and making me walk back to Fort Union."

"It would do you good," Kay said.

"Is that so?" Irene snapped.

She took a step forward and her little hands clenched. Kay held her ground, taller than Irene by at least three inches and infinitely more calm and controlled now. She gave an impression of strength, of capability. Her eyes never left Irene's features and gradually she saw the impulse of rashness fade from Irene's eyes.

"As long as you've butted in here," Kay said, "I'm going to put you to work."

Irene placed her hands on her slim hips, defiant again.

"Try it and see what happens. I'll go to Captain Sumner."

"You'll be wasting your time."

"Why?"

"Because Captain Sumner is in charge of the armed escort only. But I'm running this boat."

An unpleasant sneer lifted the corner of Irene's upper lip.

"I can see how much you're going to like ordering me around."

Kay said, "I don't like it at all. But I'll give it to you straight so there will be no misunderstanding. *The Queen* was sent up the Yellowstone with a special job to do. I'm out to see that it is done the best way I know how. Every deckhand on board has his work to do, and every soldier in Captain Sumner's detail has the individual responsibility of helping to protect the boat. Since you're here, you'll work, too. I propose to send you to the galley to assist the cook."

Irene straightened. The pale skin drew tight over her cheekbones.

"I won't do it," she said.

"Can you tell me anything else you're equipped to do?" When Irene didn't reply Kay said quietly, "All right. Either you work in the galley or stay locked up in one of the cabins. Take your choice."

The glances of the two girls clashed, seeming to shimmer like the flash of naked sabres in the sun. It was Irene who backed down.

She nodded in mute rage, then walked past Kay to the deck. She waited for Kay to close the cabin door and together they moved on to the galley.

The succeeding days found *The Queen* steaming steadily up the Yellowstone. Again and again they struck treacherous shallows where they had to resort to the spars. And all the time the timber growing along the river banks grew sparser. Kay often found it imperative to lay over for a half day while the deckhands, accompanied by a detail of soldiers, scoured along the shore for wood to cut and split into logs for the boiler fires.

Accordingly, it took the better part of a week for *The Queen* to reach the rendezvous spot. They got there early in the afternoon of the sixth day and tied up along the bank a few yards from the entrance to Glendive Creek.

As a precaution Captain Sumner sent a small party of soldiers ashore to scout the area. They returned in an hour with the news that they had picked up some Indian tracks a few miles to the east. Kay was on the promenade deck beside Sumner when the scouts brought in their report.

"That's in the direction from which Macy's column will be coming," Kay said quickly.

Sumner, a quiet, serious-faced man in his middle thirties with a neatly trimmed black moustache, nodded sombrely. He looked faintly disturbed.

"How old was the sign?" he asked the sergeant who had commanded the scout detail.

"Three—four days," said the noncom. "Hard to tell, sir."

"Moving in what direction?"

"North and south, sir. Just a small party."

"Bucks?"

"Yes, sir. No women and children—at least, not from the sign they left."

"A war party, then," said Kay, a momentary shadow crossing her face.

"It looks that way," agreed Sumner. He felt the silent strike of the sergeant's eyes and of the other soldiers who lingered nearby on the deck. "I wonder where those redskins are now and—" He broke off.

"How long it will take them to find out we are here?" Kay finished bluntly.

"Well—yes."

"I'll make a guess it won't be long," Kay said. She turned away and moved to the rail. For a few seconds she stared down at the sluggish yellow water that rolled past the packet. A frown gathered between her eyes and she looked at the distant bank before swinging back to Captain Sumner.

"What's the matter?" the officer asked, sensing a new disturbance in her manner.

"I'm thinking we may soon have another problem on our hands. The river."

"The river?" Sumner repeated, his voice bewildered.

"Yes. It's very shallow and if this dry spell continues you can expect the depth of the river to fall an inch—maybe more—a day. We might get stuck here if Macy's column is delayed. The Sioux would like that very much."

The next week seemed interminable to those aboard *The Queen*. Each day dawned bright and cloudless and summer's intense heat shimmered all around them. The decks became too hot to walk on. Inside the cabins the air was stale and lifeless.

Each day Captain Sumner sent a detail along the shore on scout patrol, and each day when Kay peered over the side of the packet she saw that the channel had gone down a little bit more.

There had been no further signs of Sioux, but the very absence of signs was somehow alarming. No one was allowed to venture far from the packet and the strain of waiting grew until it was like a great invisible blanket smothering them all.

At the end of the second week Kay decided to load *The Queen*'s freight decks with wood in case the cavalry column returned and the necessity arose for a fast trip downriver. She discussed the plan with Captain Sumner and he agreed with the wisdom of it.

Accordingly, all the deckhands were dispatched ashore, armed with axes and saws. Sumner himself commanded the detail of soldiers that went with the wood crew. Only a dozen soldiers were left behind to guard the packet.

Kay and Irene, drawn together by their mutual need of company, spent most of the afternoon on deck, watching the wooded shore that stretched away from the winding river. Some of the hostility that had existed between the two girls had evaporated. Now, though they did little talking, they shared a common anxiety.

They constantly watched the brush. But nothing

175

stirred that thick green wall of trees and bushes. There wasn't even a breeze. A deathly stillness hung in the air. The heat remained, lingering and oppressive.

Then a faint rattle of gunfire off to the west brought Kay and Irene to their feet. They rushed to the rail, looking toward the trees. The soldiers on the lower deck sprang to attention.

"Sounds like the Sioux have jumped the wood-cutting crew," yelled the burly sergeant in command.

The firing continued, far off, but sharply clear in the twilight air. The sergeant barked an order and the soldiers took up their carbines and marched ashore. The sergeant paused halfway down the gang-plank to shout a few hurried words to Kay.

"We're going in there to see if we can help. You'll be all right here."

The last sentence was uttered in the form of a question and he waited while Kay nodded and said, "Go ahead. Don't worry about us."

The sergeant grinned and ran down to join the detail. At once they vanished among the trees.

Tug Willison approached the rail. He stood beside Kay and Irene while they watched the last blue-coated soldier go twisting into the brush. For a few minutes the noise of the detail's progress was carried back to them by a faint breath of wind. Then the dead, haunting stillness settled upon the clearing, broken only at sporadic intervals by the far-off rattle of gunfire.

Fifteen minutes passed slowly by. The sound of guns seemed to move farther away.

The sun sank behind a low bank of clouds. A hint of premature darkness flowed across the river. The trees, too, seemed darker now. Shadows lengthened along the slopes of the far hills. Kay began pacing up and down the deck. She came back to Irene at the rail and the dark-haired girl turned to her with a tight, desperate look on her face.

"They shouldn't have gone off and left us here," she said.

"We'll be all right," said Tug Willison without emotion.

"Sure, Irene," Kay added with a conviction she did not feel.

There was a dull throbbing at her temples. She closed the fingers of her right hand, squeezing the tips tightly against her palm until the fingers formed a hard ball of flesh and bone.

She felt terribly alone. She knew Irene was looking to her for strength, for reassurance, and she couldn't give it to her. For the first time that she could remember she was not sure of herself. She kept watching the dark green wall of chaparral. Nothing stirred behind the foliage, yet something unnamed, something evil, seemed to vibrate in the air around the trees.

Tug Willison looked calm enough, yet he was also watching the trees with an odd concentration. They compelled and drew his scrutiny just as they held the attention of Kay and Irene. There was a dryness in Kay's mouth and throat that had not been there before. She recognized it for what it was—panic—yet she was helpless to do anything about it.

It was a feeling that spread within her, occupying all the facets of her mind. It chilled her blood, left her aching and empty.

"Oh, I wish they would come back," Irene said, her voice dangerously shrill.

The shock of her words was like a gunshot exploding in the taut silence. Kay tore her hands away from the rail and swung around. Irene looked at her out of eyes that held the deep shadow of dread. She pleaded for an answer from Kay. But there was nothing to say. And so they all turned back to the trees that were so full and thick and somehow menacingly secretive.

A pale purple light filled the clearing. The sun dropped below the horizon. Greyness, shot through with bands of mauve and pink, still filled the sky. But off to the east a pack of night clouds were gathering. Kay saw them sweeping into the west and knew that full darkness would soon be at hand.

The crackle of brush brought the three people on the deck of *The Queen* instantly alert. Tug

Willison drew his gun. Kay slid one hand into the pocket of her blue dress and fondled the carved grip of a small derringer she carried there.

The sound of men running became louder and louder. Then a group of a half-dozen soldiers broke from the trees. They were followed by eight more running figures, carrying rifles and Colts.

The sight of those blue uniforms brought a sudden easing of the tight wall of tension that had surrounded Kay and Irene. Kay dropped the derringer back in her pocket. Tug Willison grunted in pleasure and slid his Colt back in the holster.

There was an indistinguishable shout from shore. The running soldiers waved and moved on toward the gang-plank. It was impossible to make out the faces of any of the men clearly as darkness closed down upon the land.

"I wonder where the rest of them are," said Willison. "Looks like the guard detail that stayed with us until a half hour ago."

"They'll be along soon, no doubt," said Kay.

Willison moved to the companionway and hurried down to the freight deck to greet the returning soldiers. Kay and Irene, holding their skirts above their ankles, descended the steps after him.

The gang-plank echoed to the thump of running feet as the soldiers clambered aboard.

"Glad you're back," said Willison. "We were—"

He broke off at the same instant that Kay caught sight of the tall man at the head of the detail and cried out:

"Jack Wade!"

Things happened with startling swiftness after that. Willison, not recognizing any of the soldiers who rushed headlong toward him, made a belated grab for his holstered gun. Wade laughed harshly, swung his carbine around, and shot Willison point-blank in the chest.

Willison's fingers seemed to be frozen around the stock of his gun. He made a powerful effort to pull the barrel clear, staggering a few steps toward Wade. Then all the energy drained out of him and he pitched to the deck.

Kay moved even faster than Willison. Now that uncertainty was gone, she was hard and sure of what she had to do. The derringer flipped into her hand. There was a spurt of flame. Wade cursed as a bullet tore at the flesh of his upper arm. Then he threw himself at Kay. He slapped his arm against Kay's wrist, knocking the derringer to the deck, and the weight of his body striking her left shoulder drove her back against the deck housing.

All this time Irene stood rooted and motionless, her eyes wide pools of surprise and fear.

"Jack . . . Jack Wade," she murmured in a dull whisper.

Wade turned, noticing her for the first time. He

smiled thinly, his light blue eyes mirthless and sardonic.

"Irene Nostrum," he said. "This is a pleasure. No gun?"

She shook her head mutely, then turned to stare at Kay who had recovered and now completely ignored Wade to kneel beside Willison. When she got up there was a steely look in her eyes.

"You've killed him," she said to Wade.

He shrugged. "The fool shouldn't have tried to draw on me." He glanced back toward the trees and then up and down the deck. "Where's the rest of the crew?"

"Go and see," Kay said.

A bearded man standing beside Wade lifted his eyebrows and said, "Shall we look around?"

"No, Garvin," said Wade. "If this shooting didn't bring the deckhands out, nothing will. I reckon they're all out with that wood-cutting crew. We've got to get out of here before those soldiers come back. By now they've probably discovered they've been tricked and that they've been battling white men dressed up as Indians."

He swung around to Kay, handed his carbine to Garvin and drew his short gun.

"Lead the way to the pilothouse, Kay. We're moving out."

"This packet is staying right here," she retorted hotly, planting herself in front of the companionway.

181

Wade was a handsome man with a carefree, devil-may-care manner. His eyes looked languid and easy as he smiled at Kay, but there was a black glint in them.

"Garvin," he said, "get down in the engine room. I want some steam and I want it fast." He turned back to Kay, grabbed her roughly. She fought him with both hands until he slapped her across the face. "You're making it hard for yourself," he snapped. "I'll run her myself. But you're going up in the pilothouse. You, too, Irene."

He thrust the gun into Kay's ribs, forced her to lead the way up to the promenade. Two other men, dressed in the uniforms of Union soldiers, grabbed Irene and forced her to go along.

Ten minutes later *The Queen* slid away from the bank and steamed on up the Yellowstone past Glendive Creek.

Chapter 16

Five troopers collapsed on the forced march to Glendive Creek. One of them died, after an hour of agony, and Macy held up the column long enough to bury him and then they moved on.

The night had been long and terrible. The men,

aching in every bone of their bodies, weary to the point of utter exhaustion, were unable to find respite in sleep because of the nagging pressure of their thirst. In desperation Macy had collected all the canteens. But when they were pooled together there was hardly more than a mouthful for each man.

At four in the morning they were on the march, anxious to escape the searing assault of the sun's heat. By noon they had left a half-dozen of their horses behind and the mounts remaining were thoroughly spent.

They were a shapeless, bedraggled lot—a serpentine line of hunched figures, uniforms stained grey with alkali—that wound slowly and with great effort through the tangled maze of malpais that separated them from the Yellowstone.

They were like automatons, moving aimlessly on, without purpose, without any interest showing in their gaunt, dust-lined faces. Now and then a head lifted and bloodshot eyes peered around at the grey-brown ridges of earth and rock that cluttered their line of march. Then the head would tip down again and the rider would give himself up to the silent contemplation of his own misery.

Ranging ahead of the column as usual, Bill Horn cut plenty of Indian sign, but none of the tracks were recent. It was obvious that Sioux were in the region and Horn knew, as surely as he'd ever known anything, that Indian warriors were following their progress.

At noon, when they were still several hours' ride from Glendive, General Macy halted the column. Horn and Lieutenant Haggard rode back to talk with Macy. All the officers were gathered around the commander. The troopers, dismounted now, had been given permission to eat some of the meagre dry rations still remaining in their saddle bags. But few of them made any attempt to do so. Their throats were too dry and too thick to swallow any solid food.

"How far now?" Macy asked bluntly when Horn climbed down from the saddle and strode up to the group.

"Two—three hours more," Horn said.

Breadon flung a nervous glance toward the parallel ridges that stretched on either side of them.

"I wish the damned redskins would attack and get it over with," he said. "Anything is better than this waiting—this knowing they're stalking us every step of the way."

"Yeah," added Haggard. "Just waiting for the kill."

"Enough of that talk," snapped Macy. "Let them come when they please. We'll give them hell."

Haggard looked at the sprawling shapes of the troopers and shook his head. Each of those men was in his own private hell. How much fight was left in the regiment he did not dare to guess. There couldn't be a great deal more than the will to survive. And even that instinct must have been dulled by the strain and torture of these last few days.

He saw how empty and meaningless were Macy's words when he caught the pinched, beaten look on Macy's face. The commander did not believe his own words and it was clear to him that his officers did not believe them either.

Two and a half hours later the cavalry column crossed a wide boulder field, dotted here and there with clumps of mesquite and catclaw, and came to a low bluff. At the base of the bluff a cold spring bubbled out of the earth and tumbled in a crystal glitter into a shallow pool which, in turn, formed a narrow stream that vanished off into a tangle of brush.

Horn and Haggard halted there, waited for the column to come up. There was a hoarse shout from the troopers in the leading companies. Heads lifted and bodies straightened in dusty saddles.

"Better block off the pool just to be safe," advised Horn to General Macy. "Water looks all right, but you never can tell. However, the Indians can't have done anything to the spring itself."

He reined his horse around. Macy called him back.

"Where are you going?"

"Scout ahead to the top of the next ridge. We're right close to the river now. I want to see if *The Queen* is waiting for us."

As if the very mention of the possibility that Kay's packet might not be waiting at the appointed rendezvous suddenly called up a dormant fear that had been pushed back into the dim recesses of their minds, Macy and his officers stiffened to attention. All at once a strange sense of foreboding hit them. The feeling was passed along to Horn and a freezing excitement took hold of his nerves.

He spurred away from the group that now lined up around the spring. He heard the clatter of hoofs that told him Haggard was following, but he didn't look back. A sick dread stirred up his insides. It was a feeling that had been within him increasingly during this last week, yet he had thrust it aside in the compelling pressure of his own troubles. Now it could no longer be denied.

It drove him at a frenzied gallop up the grade, though his horse laboured at every step and twice came dangerously near to falling. At last he reached the crest of the ridge. Below him stretched more rocks, a dense curtain of bush and trees. And beyond the trees flowed the Yellowstone. He followed its twisting course past Glendive Creek and a lightning stab of shock whipped through him when he found the river empty. There was no sign of *The Queen*.

Although the vague, premonitory fear that something might keep Kay's packet from reaching Glendive had disturbed him frequently, the cold reality of the steamboat's absence came as a staggering blow. And he wasn't only thinking of the danger to the troops which had been relying on *The Queen* for fresh supplies. He was also thinking of Kay Graham and wondering with an all-consuming dread what had happened to her.

Once more he scanned the river with anxious eyes, unwilling to fully credit the terrifying evidence of his senses.

A sibilant whisper of sound drilled past his face. It was followed by the sharp report of a rifle. Automatically he reached for the carbine in the special scabbard beneath the stirrup fender. He was swinging the weapon in front of him when two more shots crashed out.

Below him the trees erupted into ugly life. Out of a hundred nooks and crannics in the brush poured the reddish brown figures of Sioux warriors. Horn saw at once that it was Wild Horse, the rugged Sioux chief, who was leading this Indian band. The big, steel-muscled Sioux, his mahogany-coloured face crisscrossed by narrow stripes of war paint, let out a yell when he spotted Horn, and the carbine in his hand spat flame.

A puff of dust jumped up under the front hoofs of Horn's gelding. He paused to bring his own weapon to his shoulder and fire at Wild Horse.

But the Indian chieftain was coming at a great gallop up the long grade and the bullet went wide of its mark. Horn wheeled the gelding around and sped back the way he had come.

Down the far side of the ridge Horn rode at a breakneck pace. He sent up a long yell as a warning to the column clustered about the spring below him. But he saw that the troopers had already spread out in an irregular skirmish line.

One or two soldiers, still fumbling with their canteens near the pool, dropped them in a frenzy and made a run for their horses. Macy was waving his arms and issuing curt orders. Officers were riding up and down the line as Horn skidded the gelding to a halt.

"This is it!" he yelled to the general.

"How many Sioux?" Macy demanded.

"Several hundred—maybe more. Didn't stop to count them."

Macy turned to Lieutenant Haggard.

"Spread the word for the men to dismount. Count off. Every fifth man hold the horses."

Haggard rode away. Without waiting for orders, Horn spurred off in the opposite direction, relaying the general's order.

All down the line men swung to the ground, carbines in hand. Each fifth man sprang forward to grab the reins of the horses and draw them to the rear out of range. The troopers fanned out in a double row, spreading wide. Some were able to take refuge behind rocks. Others remained in the open, set and waiting for the Indians to reach the crest of the ridge.

They came a minute later in a reddish brown wave that seemed to flow like mud down the slope of the hill. A sheet of flame preceded them. Here and there a trooper dropped, hit by a bullet.

"Fire at will!" yelled Macy and the order was passed along.

Now cavalry carbines added their roar to the violent din of sound that filled the air. Volley after volley went crashing into the Sioux ranks. Indians and horses went down in that wild charge, but their places were taken by other warriors hurrying into the breach.

For a time it seemed that Wild Horse meant to ride right over the cavalry column. Horn tensed himself, tugged at his Colt to be ready for fighting at close quarters. He saw Macy and Breadon and Haggard do likewise. Then, at the last minute, Wild Horse lifted his hand and the Indians split in two big wedges, one group swinging to the right, the other to the left.

A pall of smoke hung over the ground. Naked red forms lay sprawled all the way up and down the slope. Here and there a horse whinnied in pain. Troopers were down, too. A man who had been standing right alongside of Horn was dead with a bullet in his neck. Another lay grovelling on the ground, hands pressed to his side.

"They're going to try to encircle us!" Horn warned Macy. He watched Wild Horse's braves go riding parallel to the column's skirmish line. Then there was a new shout to the right. More Indians were pouring out of another pocket in the hills in that direction. They, too, were fanning out, making a bid to get behind the cavalry.

"To horse!" shouted Macy above the din of spitting carbines. "Fall back!"

The men fired another volley into the Sioux, then ran back at a trot. Word had been flashed back to the horse-holders. Now they came racing forward. Soldiers broke ranks and grabbed their horses, leaped into their saddles.

A renewed burst of firing came from the Sioux as they began to close in. Here and there a cavalry horse went down, carrying its rider with it. The Sioux were pressing hard, eager to finish this.

"We've got to make for that boulder field back a ways—if we can," said Horn in a tight voice.

Macy nodded grimly and hefted himself into the saddle. A red-faced private hurried up to Horn with the gelding and Horn clambered aboard. He lingered a moment to pour several more shots from his carbine into the yelling horde of Indians. He had the satisfaction of seeing two braves jackknife from their ponies and go sprawling in the dust. Then he was in full retreat with the rest of the column.

The Indians were pinching them in from three sides now, steadily narrowing the corridor of escape. Macy, Horn, and Haggard stayed with the rear guard, rallying the men whose job it was to keep the Indians back to allow the main body of troops to reach the boulders.

The smell of heat and dust and gunpowder and blood was in the air. Men shouted and screamed. The ground shook to the pounding of galloping hoofs. Breadon, riding hard on a big black gelding, brought a couple of dozen men to aid the hard-pressed right sector of the line.

Smoke and dust obscured much of the action, but Horn could see that the Sioux were hammering close in that quarter. Their fire was a wicked swath, cutting through the blue-jacketed troops. Horn raced over with more men to help. The added strength beat back the Sioux for a moment. They broke their charge, drew back to reform.

"Fall back! Fast!" yelled Horn and the order was taken up and repeated by Breadon.

The troopers reined their mounts about and raced for the boulders. They had balked the Indians' manœuvre to cut in behind them. But the margin had been unpleasantly close.

A good half of the regiment was filtering through the rocks when the Sioux came on again. Horn was lashing the last bit of speed from his jaded horse when he saw Breadon lurch in the saddle. He knew at once that the lieutenant had been hit. Breadon made a wild grab for his saddle horn, missed it, and hurtled to the ground. He landed on his shoulder, rolled over once. Immediately he got to his knees, fighting a dizzy blackness.

Horn pulled his gelding around and raced back to Breadon. He left the saddle with a bound, the force of his rush carrying him against Breadon and knocking him flat on his face. He took one brief look at the dark, hurtling forms of the Sioux weaving toward him in the clouds of dust, then thrust his arms around Breadon.

The lieutenant's eyelids flickered weakly, but there was no slackening of hostility in his manner.

"Don't try being a hero for my sake, Horn," he said thickly.

Horn ignored him, staggering to his feet with the full weight of the lieutenant's body in his arms. He stumbled to the waiting gelding, heaved him belly-down across the saddle, and jumped up behind him.

"Go on. L-leave—me," muttered Breadon.

Horn didn't even hear him. The thud of hoofs, the shrill yells of the Indians, beat in solid waves of sound against his eardrums. He dug his heels into the gelding's flanks. The animal leaped forward. A bullet whined dangerously close. Somewhere to the left there was a rattle of gunfire. Horn twisted about and saw two more blue-clad figures leave their saddles and fall to the dust.

Brush and scattered rocks drifted by as the gelding travelled at a labouring gallop toward the boulder field. Horn had his grim moment to wonder how long the horse would last carrying double in its jaded condition. Foam ringed its muzzle and its heaving sides were ribboned with dust and sweat. There was a faltering unevenness in its stride.

A hundred yards, then two hundred, they raced. And at every step Horn felt the nervous quivering of his back muscles waiting for the smash of Sioux lead. His nerves screamed with the taut expectancy of it. But it was the gelding that took an Indian bullet.

Horn knew it when the animal lurched and almost went to its knees. He slipped his feet from the stirrups, ready to jump with Breadon. Then the animal recovered and went on. But its pace was slower now, its stride ragged and fumbling.

Horn could see the blue lines of men forming ahead of him at the first row of granite rocks. He saw the puffs of smoke blossoming from the cavalry carbines and knew the troopers were firing over his head at the pursuing Indians and yet it seemed that he would never reach them.

Other blue-clad forms were thundering along beside him, anxious to reach the same haven of safety. There was blood in the foam around the gelding's muzzle. The animal was going on pure heart and spirit now. It was done for. Horn realized that and set himself.

Twenty yards from that foremost blue line the gelding went down. Horn dropped to the ground on the right side, away from the sprawling horse. He took Breadon with him, pulling him forward, and collapsed under the lieutenant's limp weight.

He was rising again when a half-dozen troopers surrounded him and took Breadon off his hands. Under a protective volley of rifle fire the rescue detail carried Breadon behind the lines and into the lee of several huge boulders where several more wounded men lay.

Chapter 17

Three minutes after the column reached the boulder field the Indian attack wavered and broke up. Macy had deployed his men cleverly in the few moments that had been allowed him before the Sioux braves swept close to their lines. The troopers abandoned their horses and hid behind rocks or bushes, fighting in true Indian fashion.

With the light fast fading in the sky and with few distinct targets to shoot at, the Indians drew back out of range. The retreat gave Macy's hard-pressed forces a much-needed respite.

A half-dozen cavalrymen, caught at the rear of the retreat, made a valiant bid to reach the boulders but were cut down by Sioux bullets. Other blue-coated shapes littered the ground beyond the regiment's line of defence. But the toll of Sioux warriors had been much heavier.

Macy, however, took scant encouragement from this circumstance, for during the brief skirmish he had seen enough to realize that Wild Horse's band outnumbered his own small command by a ratio of two to one.

Now he alerted half of the men, stationing them at strategic points around the huge amphitheatre, with orders to ready themselves for another attack. Those pack animals that had not wandered away in the confusion of the fight were now herded together. More carbine ammunition was broken out and distributed to the men.

Horn trudged wearily back to the rocks behind which Lyle Ferriss, the medical officer, had set up a crude hospital. Ferriss was in his shirt sleeves. His hands and arms were crusted with sweat and blood. Fifteen soldiers were wounded. Two or three were groaning and calling for water.

Half a dozen canteens were piled in a heap near Ferriss' kit of instruments. An orderly moved to the pile and unscrewed the cap from one of the containers. Then he went to one of the wounded men and held the canteen to the man's lips. The soldier drank eagerly, trying to clutch the canteen itself. But the orderly allowed him only a few swallows, then pushed him gently back.

Ferriss saw Horn and said with a frown, "Our old trouble. Water."

"No chance to fill up all the canteens at the spring, I suppose," said Horn.

"Hardly half the troops got water." Ferriss wiped his face with a coloured bandanna. "We can't hold out long here without it. Our one chance is *The Queen*. If that half company of infantry can divert the Indians just long enough for us to get to the spring—"

"Don't count on it," said Horn, the memory of the stark emptiness of the Yellowstone returning to him with a sharp stab of dismay. "The packet is gone."

"What's that?" demanded General Macy, coming up behind Horn. "*The Queen* isn't at Glendive?"

Horn squared slowly around to face the harassed commandant.

"No sign of it, sir. I had a good look at the river before the Sioux jumped me. The packet was gone."

"My God!" exploded Macy. "What could have happened?"

"I wish I knew."

"Maybe Wild Horse has another band of

warriors around here," said Ferris, gloomily. A feeble call from one of the wounded troopers pulled him away and he went off.

"That's what I'm afraid of," said Macy. "If the Sioux have that packet we're really cut off."

Another voice spoke behind them.

"I figure we can't be much worse off than we arc now."

Horn and Macy turned to see Lieutenant Haggard pointing to the bluffs that surrounded their position. Above them Sioux were climbing the shaly slopes. Their intent was immediately obvious.

The boulder field formed a great natural bowl. To the west the land spread out in a broad plain that rose in gradual ascent towards the hills that clustered along the shore of the Yellowstone. But directly to the north and south the ground heaved up sharply in a series of terraced, heavily wooded buttes.

Once the Sioux reached these high benches they would be in an excellent position to fire down upon the soldiers. The rocks would offer scant protection for Macy's men. To the east lay the barren trail back to the Little Missouri. Even this road was cut off now, for Wild Horse had sent a strong detachment of braves to seal the exit. The remainder of the Sioux force, still hundreds strong, was gathered in a compact group several hundred yards away.

At an abrupt signal from Wild Horse the Sioux charged the rocks once more. Macy, Horn, and Haggard darted forward. Soldiers who had been allowed to take their ease were called up. Carbines rattled, boots pounded the hard-packed ground, as the soldiers hastily resumed defensive positions.

Wild Horse led his warriors in the bold dash. He made a powerful, compelling figure as he rode his wiry paint pony straight toward the rocks. There was a brutal grin on his brown face. His rifle roared steadily.

A trooper went down, drilled through the head. Horn lifted his carbine and levered a snap shot at Wild Horse. The chief lurched forward, grabbed the mane of his pony, then straightened. A reddish stain coloured his dark skin. But he stayed aboard the paint pony, still firing.

The Indians came to within thirty yards of the soldiers before they swerved and galloped away along the far edge of the cliff. A withering spray of bullets raked their ranks, finding many targets. More and more empty horses mingled with the reckless charge.

Then, just as Wild Horse called an end to the assault, bullets began to rain down upon the troops from the crest of the bluffs. The Sioux, working their way up the slope, were finding vantage points along the bench from which they were able to subject the entire bowl to a deadly crossfire.

To counteract the Indians' move, Macy selected a group of sharpshooters, established them in protected crannies among the rocks, and ordered them to concentrate on picking off the Sioux as they climbed up to the bench.

The sharpshooters caught about a dozen Sioux in that fashion. Then the superior position of the Indians who had gained the top of the bluff forced the soldier sharpshooters to retreat. Three of the troopers were wounded and had to be dragged to safety. A fourth was literally cut in two by a hail of slugs.

From both sides of the bowl the Indians now cut loose with their carbines. There was hardly any place in the boulder field that was completely protected from the attack. In fact, Lyle Ferriss had the unpleasant experience of seeing one of the wounded troopers killed by an Indian sniper's bullet while he was in the act of probing with a scalpel for another slug that had previously lodged between two of the victim's lower ribs.

Crawling into a deep pocket between two parallel rows of rocks, Horn found General Macy conferring with Lieutenants Haggard and Lowell.

"Gentlemen, we're in a tight spot," Macy said with grave concern.

"Yes, sir," said Lowell. "Those bluffs give Wild Horse a tremendous advantage."

"We're like ducks on a pond," Haggard added, his rugged features grey and indistinct in the fast-gathering dusk. "They can cut us to ribbons as they please. And with darkness coming on—"

"I wouldn't worry about the darkness," said Horn quickly. "In fact, the Indians will stop firing when it gets dark."

"Do you think so?" Macy demanded.

It was oddly incongruous to see the tall, dark-haired commandant sprawled uncomfortably among the rocks. With his long sideburns and the dark moustache that had become ragged during their two weeks' march he suddenly looked as young as the two officers beside him and slightly unsure of himself.

"I'd almost bet on it," said Horn. "Indians don't care much for night fighting. And in this particular instance they have nothing to gain by it. In the dark, at hand-to-hand fighting, they'd stand to lose as many men as ourselves. But to-morrow, in full daylight and with those bluffs to fire from, they'll be able to see what they're shooting at and will really give us hell."

"That's what I'm worried about—to-morrow," said Macy. He rose from his crouched position, stared up at the nearest bluff now almost completely lost in shadow. The gunfire was tapering off. At the eastern end of the boulder field the Sioux were making preparations to camp. "Only thing to do right now is to get out the entrenching tools and dig in as deeply as we can behind the rocks."

200

"The men are in bad shape for that kind of work, sir," said Haggard.

Macy nodded, his jaw hard with anger. "Damn it, you're absolutely right. The last two days of forced marching with only a few swallows of water was a tough grind for everyone." He waved his arm in a savage circle. "And this just about finishes everything." Once more he stopped and this time his eyes lifted to the dark, irregular contours of the bluff. "If there were only some way of routing those red devils out of there."

Horn and the two cavalry officers joined Macy out in the open. The gunfire had ceased altogether now. Far off to the east an Indian camp-fire threw its ruddy brilliance against the thickly flowing night.

"Maybe there is a way," murmured Horn.

"How?" snapped Macy irritably. "If you have any ideas, let's hear them."

Horn answered briskly. "I noticed that there's a lot of brush up on those bluffs. Most of it is dry as tinder. With the wind blowing in the right direction a strong fire travelling toward the centre of the bowl would drive the Sioux right over the edge of the cliff."

"How do you propose to get up there?" Lowell asked, his lanky, loosely coupled figure in a weary slouch. He looked down and now that the pressure of actual fighting was over he had time to think about being thirsty again. "We'd have to break through the Sioux lines to get around to the approaches to either of those bluffs."

"The only way is to climb up the face of one of those bluffs the way some of those Indians did," said Horn promptly.

Macy shook his head. "It's no good. It wouldn't work."

"Besides, by this time," chimed in Lowell, "Wild Horse has probably sent a big bunch of his braves around to the far ends of those bluffs to reinforce his men up there."

"If he has, that's all the more reason for us to make the attempt to burn one bunch out," insisted Horn. He broke off to test the direction of the night breeze. "The wind is coming out of the north now. If we wait till the Sioux have bedded down for the night a few of us might be able to climb the face of the cliff and sneak around behind them."

"What about carbines?" asked Lowell. "You'd never climb either of those bluffs, lugging a rifle. You'd have to rely on your sidearms."

"That's all I figure we'd need up there—if we make it at all," said Horn. "It's certainly worth a chance. We know what we can expect in the morning if we wait for the Sioux to renew their attack."

Lowell made no reply. Macy, too, was silent, his attention soberly directed toward the almost perpendicular wall that towered above the boulder field. Horn, recognizing the general's silence for a weakening of his opposition, pressed his argument.

"Let me try it, sir," he said. "Assign two or three men to go along and maybe we'll give those red varmints something to think about."

Macy's answer came slowly. "I'll have to ask for volunteers. I wouldn't order any soldier on this job. It would be like signing a man's death warrant."

"To-night or to-morrow—it doesn't make much difference," said Horn. And, curiously enough, that was the way he felt. He was fully aware of the danger involved in the undertaking. Yet, as always in moments of great stress, a compelling reckless-ness had hold of him. It was a driving force that could not be denied. He added simply, and with no attempt at heroics: "If my number is up, I'd rather go out carrying the fight to the other fellow than waiting for him to pot me at his leisure."

"All right, Horn," said Macy crisply and with a sudden return of spirit. "Make your try. When do you figure on going?"

"Not until after midnight. That'll give me a whole hour until moonrise. We've got to wait until most of those Sioux warriors are asleep, but once the moon is up we'd be picked off in no time by the Indian guards on the opposite bluff. If we can circle around the Sioux camp, my idea is to hide in the brush the rest of the night. Near dawn we start the fire. If it gets a good hold, the fire should sweep through that dry grass and trap the Sioux. Their only way out will be to jump down to our camp. And the steep drop is enough to kill every redskin that tries it."

"True enough," admitted Macy. There was a distinct spark of hope, of animation, in his talk now. "You pull that stunt off, Horn, and we may get through. I'll have every company ready to hit the Indians at the west end the minute the blaze takes hold. If we can make a breach—open a wedge between the bunch out there and the band on the other bluff—we'll take them." His voice dropped suddenly. Doubt returned. "We'll be cutting things mighty fine."

"Sure," Horn admitted. "But it's our one chance."

Lieutenant Haggard stepped forward in the darkness, his figure cut a solid, black wedge against the lingering trace of light in the western sky.

"With your permission, sir," he said to Macy, "I'd like to go along with Captain Horn."

"I'll make it three altogether," added Lieutenant Lowell. "You've got me believing it might be done."

"Hold on!" protested Macy. "I can't risk losing all of my officers." He paused a moment, then laid a hand on Haggard's shoulder. "All right, Haggard. You go." To Lowell he said: "Sorry,

Tom. There'll be plenty of work to do here. More than I can handle alone."

"Haggard and two more men should do the trick," said Horn, coolly calculating the risks and the magnitude of the job that lay ahead of him. "I'd tackle it alone, for one man crawling through the Sioux lines is apt to attract much less attention than four, but when that fire starts it's got to blaze up all along the bench at once and blanket the brush so none of the Sioux can break clear."

Macy agreed that it was the only possible way in which the plan could succeed at all. Then he added: "Let's get back to the lines. We'll have to set guards at all points for the night in case of a surprise attack. And those men not on sentry duty will have to get some rest. Also, Mr. Haggard and Mr. Lowell, please instruct your men as well as the other officers that no fires are to be lit to-night.

"A lot of the men did not have an opportunity to fill their canteens. Therefore, gather all the canteens again. If there is enough left to give each man a few sips see that it is passed around. Distribute additional carbine and sidearm rounds to each man to-night."

There was an eerie, unreal quality to the starlit darkness as Macy and Horn and the two lieutenants threaded their way through the rocks to the main defence positions. Soldiers huddled in groups behind boulders and clumps of rocks.

Occasionally a low moan of pain came from some wounded trooper.

The faces of the men were only vaguely distinct in the gloom, and Horn knew that more than one of them was wondering if the Sioux would strike under cover of the darkness. That Indian eyes were even now watching them and carefully charting their movements, there was no doubt. Horn found himself wishing for some clouds to dim the starlight. Too many stars often produced a grey glow that made objects visible for some distance. It was conceivable that the faint light would be sufficient to betray the position of himself and the troopers when they started their climb to the top of the bluff.

The thought drove a frigid draught of air up and down Horn's back. He sensed a gradual tightening of his muscles, then he shrugged the feeling away.

Horn experienced no difficulty in obtaining volunteers for the special midnight mission. More than a hundred troopers signified their willingness to go along. Horn permitted Lieutenant Haggard to select the two best men from his own company.

The early hours of the night dragged along in painful fashion. The men ate meagrely of their remaining rations. Few of them had any appetite, for their need of water was too great. The little they did receive only accentuated their thirst. Actually, it was barely enough to moisten their mouths and throats.

Those troopers not assigned to sentry duty sprawled out on the ground to sleep. Horn and Haggard and the two soldiers assigned to their detail also tried to snatch a few hours' rest. But to Horn sleep would not come. His mind was too alive, too crowded with thoughts of the job that lay ahead.

Accordingly, he got up well before midnight and wandered over to the rock shelter that Macy had chosen for his own private camp. Macy was awake. In fact, he was in a huddle with his orderly and a few of the other officers, including Lyle Ferriss who had come to report on the progress of the wounded.

"Ready to go?" the general asked.

"In a few minutes," said Horn. "I'm getting restless. Besides the sky seems to be a little brighter along the horizon. That moon will be coming up soon."

He waited, standing there in the darkness, conscious of the taut stillness of the night. It was almost as if the night were listening—waiting for some sound to break the unnatural quiet.

"Looks like the Sioux have bedded down for the night," said Lieutenant Lowell out of the gloom.

"It's the quiet that bothers me," said Horn. "With both camps sleeping any stray noises will carry quite a distance."

Macy cut in quickly, "I see what you mean. When you fellows start climbing, you're sure to dislodge loose rocks and stones. The Sioux will hear that and—"

There was no need for him to complete the sentence. Every man there realized what the significance of discovery would mean to the four climbers and the rest of the regiment.

"There's a way out," said Horn. "The horses are being loose-herded not far from that bluff we'll be scaling. It might help to have the horse guard stir up those broomtails a little. The racket they make will cover up the noise of our climbing."

"And it'll cover up the sounds of Sioux braves creeping up on you in the event you are seen," added Macy.

"You're right, sir. We'll have to risk it, though."

Macy made a curt gesture to Lieutenant Lowell.

"All right," he said. "You, Mr. Lowell, see Sergeant Wilkins at the corral. Tell him what we want."

"Yes, sir," replied Lowell and moved away.

Horn turned to leave also and Macy called softly after him, "Good luck, Captain."

He went back to the others and roused them. Haggard rose at once, though he had been sound asleep. The two troopers, Arley and Freon by name, rubbed sleep out of their eyes, then looked to their holstered Colts to check the bullet loads.

"Time to go," whispered Horn. "We'll keep low all the way to the bluff. Take advantage of every bit of cover you can find—and I mean bushes and rocks that will shield us from both cliffs. In a few seconds those geldings in the corral ought to start acting up."

He dropped to his hands and knees and began crawling along the ground. Behind him Haggard and the two troopers duplicated his manœuvre. It was easy to distinguish the darker blots of brush and rocks that loomed up before them.

Horn felt his heart begin to pump at an accelerated rate. It wasn't the exertion of travelling on hands and knees. It was the nagging feeling of uneasiness that stayed like a heavy weight with him. Despite a few clouds that drifted across the sky, there was still ample light coming from the galaxy of stars that cluttered the heavens. If they were spotted by the Indians—if their purpose was suspected . . . Well, they'd know when they got to the top.

The thump of pounding hoofs shook the earth nearby. Here and there a horse whinnied. A little puff of dust leaped up from the rocks that hid the corral from view. Somewhere a trooper cursed a horse and then the clatter of hoofs sounded again.

Horn crawled into an area of thick shadow. He knew then he was close to the cliff wall. He kept on until his hand struck the shaly slope. Slowly he stood up and waited for his three companions.

They came and stood beside him, panting a little from their exertions and from a nervous excitement they couldn't quite control. Horn took Haggard's arm, drew him close.

"Now the fun begins," he said in a low tone that the lieutenant barely heard. "We'll take it slow and easy. The first twenty or thirty feet of the wall is almost straight up and down. After that it slopes inward—a break for us. Test every crevice before you move. Try not to dislodge any rocks or dirt. I'll lead."

Haggard didn't answer. He merely let his hand rest on Horn's shoulder for a moment and gave it a firm squeeze.

Horn glanced at the opposite cliff once more then turned to the wall beside him and felt for a toe hold with his boot. He found one, wedged his foot into it, and hoisted himself up, groping for a new hold with his outstretched hands.

It was slow, painful work. He went up five feet, then ten, then fifteen and paused to rest. The smell of dry, dusty granite was in his nostrils. It seeped into his throat and the agony of holding back a cough almost made him lose his hold.

Below him the horses were still creating a slight racket. Faintly, too, he heard a light scuffing sound, a tinkle of falling sand, that told him Haggard and the two troopers were following as best they could.

Up again he moved, reaching for small holes in the rock facing of the cliff or for meagre out-croppings that offered a hand or foothold. He guessed that he was about forty feet from the ground when he levered his body up another notch, dug his right boot into a crevice, and suddenly felt it give way.

For a terrifying moment that stifled his breathing he thought he was finished. He hung there by his hands, waiting for the tiny ledge above him to crack and disintegrate. Blood pounded in his temples. It slogged heavily beneath his ribs. He seemed to be choking with his own blood. His arms ached until he thought they would be yanked out of their sockets. Then, his dangling, scrabbling feet struck another small rock outcropping. It was just enough purchase to support his weight.

"Horn!" came Haggard's anxious, almost inaudible whisper. "You all right?"

"Yeah," said Horn. "But watch it. There's a soft place below."

When his jumpy nerves had ceased their trembling he moved on again. Five minutes later he noticed that the pitch of the slope was less acute. It made climbing easier.

The night gradually turned brighter. Horn ventured a glance toward the horizon and saw a milky-white glow that heralded the rising moon.

A swift anxiety took hold of him then. He moved faster because of the imminent danger of discovery. Yet, as the minutes dragged on and a deadening exhaustion slowly atrophied his muscles, it seemed that he was getting no nearer to the top.

Blackness whirled before his eyes. His fingers, cut and bleeding from sharp stones, fumbled more and more in their feverish groping for new crevices.

Then, without warning, his right hand shot upward and hit nothing. Carefully he let his fingers drift downward until they struck a flat surface directly above him.

A feeling of elation hit him. This was it. He had reached the top. He stayed there, getting his breath, listening for sounds from the Indian camp. From afar off he detected a murmur of guttural voices. He had no way of knowing if any Sioux guards were patrolling this edge of the bluff. But there was only one way to go—and that was up and over the crest.

He bent his head, looked down into the shadows below him.

"Now!" he whispered.

No answer floated back and he did not know if Haggard heard him. In fact, in his brief glance he was unable to make out the lieutenant's form. For all he knew, Haggard might have fallen or gone off at a tangent along the face of the cliff. But this was no time to wait.

Horn got a firm grip on the flat rock above him, then levered his body up and over the top. For a few seconds he sprawled there on his face, panting from his efforts. The dim murmur of Indian voices still reached him. Through the screen of brush he saw a faint flicker of light marking a Sioux campfire.

There was a scraping sound below him, followed by the rattle of some stone loosened from the face of the cliff, which went tumbling down to the cavalry encampment. Horn rose cautiously, then bent over to extend a hand to Haggard climbing toward him.

He hauled the lieutenant up beside him. Then, together, they turned and helped the two troopers mount to the ledge on which they stood.

"We've got to fade quickly," said Horn, pulling Haggard behind a tangle of dusty, sun-dried chaparral.

They moved forward slowly and cautiously, sticking to the rim of the cliff as it cut backward toward the Indian campfire. Horn saw at a glance that they would have to pass dangerously near the fire to get around the Sioux warriors. Most of them were sprawled on the ground, asleep. But a few lean, brown braves crouched around the feeble flames of the dying fire. And somewhere there must be guards patrolling the bluff.

The thought had hardly entered Horn's head when Haggard stumbled over the exposed root of a sapling and fell to his knees. Haggard was picking himself up when a big Sioux brave slithered into the brush directly in front of Horn.

The Indian's hand dropped to the knife stuck in the narrow band at the edge of his breechclout. Before the glittering blade even came free Horn closed the distance between them. He hit the Indian with his shoulders, one hand clamping over his mouth, the other driving the blade of his own knife into the Indian's back.

A faint, gurgling cry spilled from the Sioux warrior's throat. He threshed about wildly in Horn's arms before the life drained out of him and Horn sent him hurtling out into empty space.

Quickly Horn whirled and shoved his hand against Haggard to signal a halt. The two troopers stopped in their tracks, crouched behind the thick brush. They were watching Haggard and Horn. The latter had drawn his Colt. Now Haggard followed suit, his body low and tense, his attention centred on the yellow glow of the campfire.

The four Sioux warriors hunkered around the fire had risen. They were looking toward the edge of the bluff and the thick screen of bushes that hid Horn and his three companions. Long knives glittered in the firelight and the white men had a swift glimpse of fierce, painted faces before the Sioux came with a silent rush toward the chaparral.

Chapter 18

When Garvin returned from his trip to the engine room of *The Queen* Wade let him take over the wheel. Two more of Wade's Jayhawkers stood guard near the door to the pilothouse. Knowing that Kay would make a break for freedom, regardless of danger, Wade had called in the men so he could give full attention to steering the packet through the winding channel of the Yellowstone.

Now he turned and strode leisurely toward Kay. There was only a little light left in the western sky and the packet was proceeding at half speed. Inside the pilothouse it was almost completely dark. But as Wade came close to her Kay saw the look of sardonic pleasure on his face.

"I reckon I'm going to need your help, Kay," he said.

"With what?" The question was flat, uncompromising.

"Didn't you know?" he asked lightly. "That bullet from your gun skinned my arm. It doesn't hurt, but it's still bleeding. I'm going to let you fix it for me."

He tugged at the torn sleeve of his blue tunic.

He ripped it all the way up to his armpit. Blood stained his shirt sleeve darkly. He tore the sleeve away, revealing a narrow strip of lacerated flesh. Blood still seeped slowly from the deep scratch.

Kay looked at the wound and lifted her eyes to Wade's face. A taunting smile lingered on his lips. It disappeared when he noticed how coldly and steadily she regarded him.

"It's time for you to turn around and tear a strip of cloth from your petticoat, Kay," he said.

"You'll wait a long time before I lift a finger to help you."

Wade's features looked a little unpleasant when he said, "I don't think you really mean that, Kay."

"No? Then I'd better put you straight. I've got no use for a Jayhawker—a man who wears the uniform of both sides in this war and robs and kills for his own personal gain. If you were wearing that Union uniform to help the cause of the South I could tolerate all this. But you're nothing but a renegade—a renegade who'd sell out his best friend for a few gold pieces."

The handsome veneer was wiped from Wade's face by a sudden mask of rage. His mouth thinned out in a hard line. He stepped close to Kay. She never moved and there was no break in the enmity of her expression.

Somehow the knowledge that she was unafraid of him drove Wade to rashness.

"Since I can't have a part of your petticoat I'll

take something else," he said and pulled her into his arms.

The change that came over her was startling. She fought Wade like a tiger. She squirmed and twisted in his embrace, lashing out with her fists, kicking at his legs. He laughed at first, enjoying her discomfort and the aroused murmurs of amusement that came from his men.

Twice he bent her head back and tried to kiss her. Each time she turned her mouth away at the last instant and his lips merely brushed her cheek. A sharp thrust from the toe of her boot drove a stab of pain along the calf of his leg. A flashing hand raked the skin of his cheek.

The laughter went out of him. He turned brutal. His arms increased their crushing pressure. The weight of his body carried her backward until her shoulders touched the wall of the pilothouse and she could go no farther. Again he bent his head. This time she could not avoid his lips. They came solidly against her own, rough and demanding.

He held Kay in that stifling embrace. His mouth dallied against hers. He took his time. He knew he was hurting her and he was fiercely glad. He waited for her to yield under that iron pressure. But her resistance never flagged. Her lips gave him nothing back.

At last he let her go. He dropped his arms. He watched her while the depth of his breathing made it difficult for him to talk.

"That was very nice," he said with an evil pleasure. "We'll have to do that again."

Kay did not bother to answer him. She was still unafraid, still unbeaten. She was breathing more rapidly than usual, but her face still held the same cold contempt.

He started to move toward her again. Irene thrust herself in front of him. A wide strip of white petticoat dangled in her fingers.

"Jack," she said, "let me fix that arm."

He grinned. "Sure, Irene."

He held his arm out while she bandaged the wound. When she had finished she asked:

"What are you going to do, Jack?"

He put a big hand under her chin, tipped her face toward him. She didn't draw back.

He said, "I'm going to kiss you, Irene. Have you any objections?"

He had his way with her lips. When he stepped back he looked at Kay and laughed. She returned his glance steadily.

Garvin called out from his position at the wheel.

"Too dark now, Jack. I reckon we'd better stop."

Wade peered through the windows. The light had gone completely from the sky. The Yellowstone was a black ribbon below them.

"All right. Ring the engine room," said Wade. "We'll lay to until the stars come out. Later, there'll be a moon. That should give us enough light to keep going all night."

One of the guards left the door and came over to the table to light one of the coal-oil lamps. He turned the wick low so that the flickering flame barely dispelled the shadows that filled the room.

"Make that light brighter," Wade told him.

"Better not, Jack," cautioned Garvin, tugging nervously at his black beard. "No sense in advertising where we are."

Wade snorted in derision. "If you're worried about that bunch of dog soldiers we tricked back near Glendive, forget about them. They'll have a tough time tracking us down on foot. And in another hour we'll be on the move."

He swung around toward Kay. A quick flare of pleased humour stirred in his eyes.

"As for Macy and your friend, Bill Horn," he said, "by this time I reckon they're fighting for their lives. Don't expect any help from them. They can't even help themselves."

It was goading talk, but Kay did not rise to it. She was conscious of a tightening of the nerves in her chest as new fear awakened in her. Still she gave no outward sign of the turmoil within her.

Irene, however, feeling no compulsion for silence or restraint asked the question that Kay was meant to ask.

"What's happened, Jack?" she said. "Tell me. Has Wild Horse attacked Macy's command?"

"Not yet. The attack is set for to-morrow and those handsome Union cavalrymen and their officers are riding into a trap. When Wild Horse springs it they won't have a chance."

Temper got the best of Kay. She said, "You seem to know a lot about Wild Horse's affairs. That means you're still partners."

"Partners?" he repeated, an amused smile on his lips.

"Why, yes," she said, "Did you forget that skirmish along the upper Missouri when Bill dynamited that herd of buffalo? Your Jayhawkers weren't much help to Wild Horse then, were they."

"You figure I was in on that?" Wade asked, still smiling.

"I wouldn't bet on anyone else." She regarded him coldly. "Better watch your step with Wild Horse. He'll turn on you some day. Then'll you be just another scalp hanging from his belt."

Savagery pinched Wade's lips together.

"That so?" he said, almost in a growl. "Wild Horse has me to thank for helping set that trap for your pretty blue cavalrymen. He's got a big band of warriors with him, but not quite enough to lick Macy in an open battle. However, I do give that redskin credit for leaving a nice broad trail for Macy to follow across the badlands of the Missouri—a trail that just made a wide circle back to the Yellowstone.

"Macy's horse soldiers probably wore themselves out trekking across the badlands in the heat. And all the while the Sioux were just leading them on, weakening them for the final kill while Wild Horse collected more braves. It was my idea to capture your packet as the Indians were jumping Macy's command. I also suggested a good spot to trap the cavalry.

"Not far from the Yellowstone there's a fresh spring that never runs dry. Beyond it is a boulder field. A strong assault by the Sioux would push those troops right into a pocket surrounded by bluffs from which a bunch of straight-shooting red varmints could really have some fun."

Anger churned inside Kay.

"And what do you get out of this?" she asked.

Wade's grin mocked her. "Why, the pleasure of seeing another bunch of Union troops slaughtered. We're still at war, you know."

Wade was being studiedly brutal. Kay knew that and fought to control her feelings.

There was a look of horror on Irene's face when she said, "But they're white men, Jack. And you're white."

"What of it?" he said sharply. "They're no friends of mine. I'm in this war for what I can get out of it." He glanced at Kay. He relished the shock that his words brought to her. She was shaken and she was angry. The rigid control of her facial muscles told him that. "I started out on the side of the Confederates. But it didn't take me long to find out who was going to win. The South hasn't a chance. Only Jeff Davis and the rest of the South don't know it yet. Meanwhile, I'm working for myself and getting rich. Does that interest you, Kay?"

A faint curl of her upper lip was the only answer Kay gave him.

Irene spoke anxiously. "Where are you taking us?"

"Just for a short trip up the Yellowstone to the Tongue River where we'll meet a small band of Sioux and hand over all the rifles and ammunition on board in return for a fortune in furs. The Sioux have the furs cached near the Tongue and they'll have horses waiting for us. After that—"

"After that, what?" Kay demanded harshly.

"Why, we'll head overland for Fort Benton, maybe. Gold has been found in Bannock and there'll be plenty of it around Fort Benton waiting to be taken. I might even make the trip by packet —after the Sioux sack Fort Union."

This information startled Kay, but she remained calm.

"It's been tried many times without success," she said.

"This time will be different," Wade told her. "Wild Horse is expecting some more Sioux lodges to join him at the Tongue. With the arms on this packet I reckon he can turn the trick. How do you think you'll like Fort Benton, Kay?"

"I won't like it because I'm not going," she snapped.

"There's nothing you can do about it, Kay," he said. "A man can get mighty lonesome travelling around in this country. You can help me pass the time."

Kay ignored the implications of Wade's remark. She said with a sudden, sharp insistence, "I'll kill you first, Jack."

He grinned. "I believe you would—if you ever got the chance."

Irene spoke up nervously. "And what about me?"

"Why, you're coming along, too," Wade told her good-humouredly. "After all, I might get tired of Kay."

Irene's lips stiffened in anger, and humiliation sent a wave of colour into her cheeks. "You devil," she said.

From the other side of the pilothouse Garvin broke into the conversation.

"Looks bright enough outside to get going again, Jack."

Wade turned away from Kay and Irene and stepped to the pilothouse windows. He stared down at the river, now faintly illumined in the star shine.

"All right, Bud," he said. "Ring the boys in the engine room for some steam. Keep it at half speed and watch the channel for shoals and sand bars."

Fifteen minutes later *The Queen* moved on

upriver at reduced speed. Garvin remained at the wheel, guiding the packet carefully through the narrow channel. They proceeded for three miles without mishap. Then they ran aground on a submerged bar.

Wade dashed to the wheel and grabbed it away from Garvin.

"Damn you, Bud!" he growled. "I told you to be careful. If we get stuck here that company of infantry will catch up with us in the morning."

Garvin cursed. "Hell, Jack, you try tooling this crate through that damned channel in the middle of the night. It isn't easy."

Wade shoved him aside. He called the engine room and ordered full speed reverse. A great trembling ran through the packet as the paddle wheel churned up a muddy foam in the shallows. Wade swung the wheel hard over and rang frantically for more steam. Again and again the craft shuddered in every timber as the paddle wheel dug into the sandy bed of the river.

Suddenly with a great sucking sound the packet slid backward into the deeper water of the channel. Wade signalled for forward speed again and this time heeled the craft sharply to port. Very slowly they went past the edge of the sand bar, cutting around it to the main channel beyond.

The experience turned Wade definitely more cautious. And even though the moon came up a few hours later, giving them more light, he finally called a halt after they came to another big sand bar. This bar stretched completely across the Yellowstone. There was no way around it. The only way left was the spars and Wade decided to wait until morning before using them.

Kay and Irene were shown to one of the cabins —Kay's own cabin, in fact—and were locked in. When they awoke shortly after dawn *The Queen* was already under way. The jolting motion of the steamboat as the spars were put into use to crow-hop the ship across the bar made sleep impossible.

Wade had breakfast brought to Kay's stateroom, then summoned both women to the pilothouse. He was in high good humour when they arrived.

"Good morning, Kay and Irene," he said. "I trust you both slept well."

Kay ignored his remark and asked bluntly, "Do you still think you're going to get away with your plan?"

"Sure, Kay," he answered. "Who is there to stop me?"

Kay regarded him with a cool, searching intensity. Something in the straight thrust of her shoulders beneath her frilly blue dress and in the determined set of her dimpled chin impelled him to add:

"If you're thinking of trying any tricks, don't do it," he warned. "Nothing is going to stop me. Not even you."

She shrugged and turned to look out of the

pilothouse window. But in the back of her mind a desperate plan was forming.

As the morning wore on and *The Queen* steamed steadily up the Yellowstone, each hour bringing them nearer to the rendezvous with Wade's Indian friends at the Tongue, Kay found herself giving the plan serious consideration.

It was hazardous and it meant the loss of the boat. Yet she realized that, in the long run, it would be no more hazardous than to allow Wade to use her and Irene as pawns in his outlaw enterprise. And she was just stubborn and strong-willed enough not to want to admit she was beaten.

Late in the afternoon *The Queen* rounded a bend in the river and Wade sighted the junction of the Tongue far ahead.

"Just about another mile to go," he shouted to Garvin. "Bud, take the wheel."

Garvin shuffled over to relieve Wade.

"The crew all set to unload the guns and ammunition on the freight deck?" Wade asked.

"Yeah. Just waiting to see Wild Horse's redskins."

"Good." There was solid pleasure showing in the rugged, handsome lines of Wade's sun-browned face. He turned to Kay. "If you've got any personal effects you'd like to take along you'd better get them because we'll be leaving *The Queen*."

226

Kay replied more quickly than she intended.

"Yes. There's a bolt of dress goods I'd like to get."

Wade laughed. "What are you going to do with that? We'll be travelling by horse overland. Won't be much chance to make a dress. Besides, I'll want to be amused."

She gave him a straight, cool look.

"Am I free to go to my cabin?"

"Sure," he said. "But I'll come along, just in case."

It was what Kay had hoped for. She wondered if her sudden nervous elation showed in her face. But Wade was still grinning, and now he pushed Kay and Irene ahead of him toward the companionway.

Below on the freight deck Kay saw several blue-clad figures lounging near some stacked cases. And far ahead a thin column of blue smoke arose in the air already growing chill with approaching night.

Kay came to the cabin and waited for Wade to unlock the door with the key he had appropriated. He let the two women precede him, then lingered behind to light the coal-oil lamp on the table.

In the flickering lamplight Kay looked suddenly tense and uneasy. Wade continued to grin.

"Go ahead, Kay," he said. "Get your things."

She nodded, fighting the rising tide of excitement within her. She walked to the corner of the cabin and bent over a small trunk. She opened the lid and fumbled inside for a moment. When she arose she was holding a huge square bolt of blue dress material. She walked toward Wade who regarded her with an air of sardonic amusement. She came within a few feet of him, then suddenly hurled the bolt of goods in his face.

He staggered backward with a muffled cry. The material clung to his face. It impeded his arms in their frantic stabbing toward the guns holstered on either hip. Then as the material dropped to the floor and billowed around his legs Kay's sharp voice cut through the stillness of the stateroom.

"Up with your hands, Jack!"

Only then did he notice the gun in Kay's hand— the gun that had been cleverly hidden under the bolt of goods. It was a nickel-plated .32 and the barrel was centred steadily on his chest.

"You damned hellcat," Wade grunted. His long upper lip flared tightly against his strong white teeth. There was passion in every word he uttered. "I'll fix you for this."

"Not to-day you won't, Jack," Kay said, her savage coolness an amazing thing to witness. "Irene and I are getting off. So are you and your renegades."

He laughed without humour. "What do you think you can do. Just one yell and a half-dozen of my men will be up here."

The gun never wavered in Kay's hand. Her

eyes were narrow blue slits, alert and quick with purpose.

"Try it, Jack," she said softly, "and see what happens."

Into the uneasy stillness came a new sound— the rasp of metal as Kay cocked the revolver.

"At this distance," she added, "I ought to be able to drive the third button of your shirt right into your chest."

Rage had its wicked way with Wade's feelings. He stood on widely planted feet, his arms at his sides, his big hands clenched, teetering on the edge of a break.

"You wouldn't dare pull the trigger," he said gruffly.

Kay's voice cut abruptly across his words. "Go for one of your Colts. You'll see how much I dare!"

"Kay!" protested Irene, startled by this turn of events. "Put that gun away. You can't do anything now. It's—"

"Shut up, Irene," said Kay. "I'm clearing off *The Queen* and I'm taking you with me."

"But—"

"Irene," interrupted Kay, her voice turning heavy with impatience, "I want you to go up behind Wade and get his guns. Take them one at a time and toss them along the floor to me. And be careful you don't get too close." To Wade she added: "I told you before to lift your hands. Now raise them above your head and keep them well away from your guns as you're doing it."

Slowly, his features contorted in a grey mask of anger, Wade raised his arms. For just the fraction of an instant his splayed fingers paused near the stocks of his guns. His hot eyes telegraphed the rash impulses that were prodding him. But he saw Kay's straight, unswerving stillness before him and he saw how her slender fingers grew white and taut about the nickel-plated .32. Then his hands and arms moved the rest of the way and shot over his head.

Irene trod uncertainly forward. She swayed as if she were going to faint. Kay's sharply intoned "Irene" made her stiffen, brought colour back to her cheeks. She came up behind Wade, fumbled for Wade's left-hand gun, and drew it clear. She drew back and skidded it along the floor to Kay. Without lowering her glance, Kay got the gun under her boot and kicked it behind her.

Irene moved around to the other side of Wade. He peered over his shoulder at her. Again he toyed with the idea of a break. Every muscle in his body quivered with the gathering tension. His eyes met Irene's and she stopped. Doubt was a grey film clouding her eyes.

"Irene, finish it," said Kay. At this moment she was the coolest one in the cabin. She took a step forward. "Never mind, I'll get the gun myself."

There was a compelling quality in Kay's voice.

It was the voice of a woman accustomed to getting her own way, of leading others. It gave Irene the needed courage to go through with it. She reached forward, got the gun and jerked it clear. Again she sent it skidding along the floor to Kay.

Wade's hands came down slowly. His chest lifted up and down to the hard run of his breathing.

"Now you've got my guns," he said, "you still have to get off the boat. That means stopping it. And what about the Sioux waiting a mile away." Confidence was coming back to him. It made him arrogant.

"I'm not worrying about stopping the packet," Kay told him. "As for the Sioux, they'll be no friends of yours when I'm finished."

Wade gave her a sharp glance. Speculation, then fear, glittered in his eyes. She was looking past him at the table—at the burning coal-oil lamp that stood squarely in the centre. A premonition of what she planned to do hit him.

She took three steps toward the table. Desperation drove him toward her. But she was fast— amazingly fast. She reached the table, threw a hand against the edge, and tilted it toward him. His legs got tangled up in the legs of the table and he fell flat on his face.

The lamp went skidding over the edge and struck the floor with a splintering crash. Coal-oil splashed into Wade's face. A tiny runnel of flame from the lamp wick darted along the trail of spilled oil. In a second the boards were afire.

Wade climbed to his feet and stamped at the flames.

"Get back!" Kay shouted.

"But Kay," Irene protested. "If we don't put the fire out the whole boat will go up in flames."

"That's what I want," said Kay grimly. "There's a small case of dynamite and caps over in the corner. When the flames hit that dynamite the boat will explode. We're getting off and so are Wade and his men unless they're fools. And Wild Horse's Sioux warriors will have to get guns from somebody else."

Angry as he was, Wade could not help admiring Kay. She stood there, straight and unyielding, watching the flames spread eagerly along the floor, knowing that she was watching the destruction of a boat that represented a small fortune to her.

Smoke began to fill the cabin. It whirled about in blue clouds. The table was fully ablaze now, the heat of it driving them toward the door. A crackling roar filled the room. One arrow of flame fled to the far wall and climbed toward the ceiling like a moving red arrow. Other runnels of flame spread fanwise toward the dark corner where a small wooden case stood.

"Let's go," said Kay.

She pushed Irene ahead of her. Irene fumbled for the door knob. In her panic the knob slid around in her moist palm. Wade shoved past her, turned the knob, and flung the door open. There was sweat on his cheeks. It clung in tiny beads to his upper lip. His eyes had a hunted look.

Irene and Wade raced toward the companionway. Kay ran after them. She realized that it would be only a matter of minutes before the flames reached the dynamite.

"We've got to stop the boat!" Irene screamed.

There was a shout from the pilothouse as Garvin, up above them, saw a black column of smoke spiral past him. But they were already clambering along the deck. They came to the companionway. One of Wade's renegades was climbing the steps. Kay fired the gun into the air, then she stepped behind Wade and struck him on the head with the barrel.

It was a hard blow, sufficient to stun him, but not enough to knock him out. He lost his balance and went tumbling down the companionway. He collided with the other man. The down-plunging weight of Wade's body sent them both hurtling to the freight deck.

Kay thrust Irene over to the rail.

"Stop the boat!" Irene screamed again.

"We're going over," said Kay.

"But I can't swim," said Irene, her eyes wide with fear.

"There's always a first time," snapped Kay and boosted Irene up to the rail.

The door of the pilothouse was flung open. Garvin yelled at them. His gun roared. A bullet sped past them. Kay fired once, driving Garvin back. Then she climbed to the top of the rail, and together she and Irene leaped over the side of the packet.

Chapter 19

Time seemed to stand still while Horn and his three cavalrymen waited for the Indians to approach their hiding place in the brush. This would end it, Horn told himself with a dismal sense of defeat. Those Sioux warriors, hunting in the chaparral for the cause of the disturbance, could not possibly fail to find them. And while he and Haggard and the others might be able to subdue these braves, they could not hope to do so without arousing the entire Sioux camp. Once that happened they were doomed.

The knowledge of what was to come was like bitter gall to Horn. A dull feeling of hopelessness seized him. He wasn't afraid to die. But he could not tolerate the thought of failure. The lives of several hundred cavalrymen depended on what occurred in the next few minutes.

Brush crackled faintly ahead of them. The Sioux were beating their way toward the bluff. Horn turned to look at Haggard. Suddenly his glance drifted to the edge of the cliff. A surge of hope beat through him.

"Back to the cliff," he said in a voice that was barely a whisper. "It's our only chance." A tree branch cracked a few rods away and Haggard crouched closer to Horn to catch the rest of his words. "If we're discovered we're licked," Horn went on. "The best bet is to swing over the cliff edge. We can climb down a notch or two and stay there, or hang by our hands from the top— and trust they don't spot us in the dark."

Haggard nodded and whispered briefly to the two troopers. Then, retreating with tremendous caution through the chaparral, they proceeded to the edge of the bluff. A few clouds had moved across the sky. They blotted out some of the stars and the yellow rim of the moon now rising along the far horizon. The darkness was intense, like a thick, cloying fog. Yet Horn was thankful for it.

He reached the cliff edge and halted. A small patch of brush struggled for existence in the dry earth. It might be just enough cover to hide their hands.

"Down we go," he said and dropped to his hands and knees.

He slid his body backward so that his legs dangled out in space. Slowly, carefully, he eased himself fully over the edge. His fingers dug into the hard dirt, seeking a firm hold. He felt the tug of his one hundred and eighty pounds. There was a solid strain under his armpits and he felt his fingers slipping.

Panic gripped him then. His fingers kept sliding. He forced his legs against the bluff, groping with the toes of his boots. He found a niche for them, dug in. He sank his left hand deeply into the dirt above him. The grit got under his nails, lacerating the flesh of his fingers. With his free hand he explored for a niche for his hands.

At last he found a slender outcropping. He leaned on it, testing its strength. It seemed solid enough so he lowered his other hand to it and let himself drop completely below the rim of the rocky bench. Beside him there was a faint scraping sound, a tinkle of loose gravel, and he saw, out of the corner of his eye, Haggard's big bulk hanging precariously by his hands.

A hot pressure of anxiety swept through Horn as he wondered if the two troopers had been able to manœuvre into suitable positions to avoid detection. The scuff of moccasined feet sounded above them. Then came an exchange of guttural words and more scraping and scuffing. The Sioux were searching the chaparral only a few feet away.

Would they come to the cliff edge? Would they lean over and spot the soldiers hidden against the wall of the bluff? These were the questions that kept whirling in Horn's brain, giving him no peace.

The Indians remained near, stamping through the bushes. Their very thoroughness was terrifying. One of them uttered a short command. Horn felt the vibration as two pairs of moccasined feet approached the rim. He waited there helplessly, his fingers aching from strain. He pressed his body close to the cliff. It was still dark, but any minute the moon might lift free of the low bank of clouds. If it did, this little expedition would be all over.

He dared not risk a glance above him. Yet he sensed that a couple of the Indians had walked to the rim. They stood there, not moving, listening for some stray sound.

Sweat was rolling down Horn's cheeks. The strain on his hands and arms became unbearable. He felt some loose grit under his fingers and realized that the outcropping he was holding on to was beginning to dissolve.

Then, when he thought he would have to move and give away his position, he heard the Indians padding along the opposite side of the bench. With the last of his strength he hoisted himself to the rim. Haggard followed his example. In a moment the two troopers also appeared.

The four men huddled together in a taut, anxious group. Horn's shirt clung damply to his chest. Every muscle in his body quivered from his recent exertions. Beside him he heard Haggard's hard-drawn breathing.

They had skinned through. But there were still more risks to be run. They had to circle behind the Sioux camp without being detected. Their chances were slim, yet there was no hesitancy in Horn's manner when he curtly waved them on.

With slow, painful caution they walked along the edge of the bluff, angling toward a rise of ground that marked the limits of the Indian camp. For the most part, the high-growing chaparral afforded them ample protection. However, in several places they were compelled to drop to their hands and knees and crawl past some low bushes.

There was no sign of the Sioux searchers. Horn surmised that they were still hunting on the other side of the cliff.

After a few moments Horn found himself opposite the dying campfire. The sprawled forms of sleeping Indians were stretched about in the grass and Horn's line of travel forced him to pass within a few feet of some of the sleepers.

This proved the most trying and difficult time for Horn and his companions. Each crawling step had to be studied in advance. The slightest scraping noise, the rasp of a stone beneath a hand, even their laboured breathing, might awaken the Indians.

But finally they got past the danger point and faded into the shadows beyond the campfire. The brush thickened rapidly except for a small grove where the Indian ponies were staked out to graze.

Horn led his small band through the bushes. Beyond the grove they rose from their hands and knees and continued at a slow, padding walk up the grade.

At the top of the slope there was a narrow bench of hard earth. On the far side the bench fell away in a steep slope that curved around toward the main trail and the high-walled canyon which harboured Macy's cavalry units.

Horn's suggestion that they hole up in the brush until near dawn met with instant approval, for their experiences of the past hour had been completely exhausting.

Weary as they were, they could do little more than doze in their uncomfortable hiding place. The heat, the smell of dust, the unremitting pangs of thirst, combined to rob them of the rest they sorely needed. They watched the moon soar upward through the sky and begin its slow, downward journey. Then as the blackness turned to grey and a faint band of light appeared low along the eastern horizon Horn called his men together.

"Time to start," he said. "Has everyone enough matches?" He waited for their confirming nods before going on. He rested his weight on one knee. His right arm was propped across the other leg while he planted his foot firmly on the ground. He gestured to the two troopers. "Arley and Freon, you men separate and go to either end of the bluff and work toward Haggard and myself. We'll start here in the middle and work outward toward you. Got that?"

"Yeah," said Arley gruffly.

"All right. Go ahead. And, remember, work fast. When this brush goes up I want it to form a solid wall of fire to block off the escape of any of those Sioux."

"Suppose some of them get through?" Haggard inquired.

"We stay back to stop as many as we can," said Horn. "The important thing is to set the fire properly so no one gets through. Hurry now before the whole camp is up."

Arley and Freon went skulking off through the brush. Horn and Haggard delayed for a few precious moments to allow the two troopers to gain their designated positions at the edges of this huge sloping mesa. Finally Horn removed a small oilskin packet from his hickory shirt. He unfolded it and drew out several matches.

Gathering a handful of dry brush stalks, he scratched a match into flame and set the stalks afire. With this improvised torch he began moving through the chaparral. The stiff dawn breeze at his back caught the first flaring sparks and carried them forward into other patches of brush. There was a crackling sound, a dull roar, then a *whoosh* as ruddy flames engulfed the bush directly in front of Horn.

He moved swiftly down the line of bushes, setting each ablaze. Far to his left he saw a burst of flames, followed by a column of smoke as Arley started his fire. And to his right other fires were born as Haggard and Freon tackled the brush on their side.

Within five minutes the wind was whipping a wicked red wall of flames down the slope toward the Sioux camp. Black smoke filled the greying sky. All along the mesa the early-morning air was alive with a savage, murmuring roar—the full-throated cry of hungry flames devouring the grass and brush in their path.

Down in the grove Indian ponies set up a frightened whinnying. There were shouts, too, as the Sioux rose from sleep and made a rush for their horses. Horn's loud yell drew Haggard and the two troopers close.

"We'll keep scattered a bit and watch for any of them to break through."

The fire rushed on toward the Indian camp, red and cruel and demanding. The grade below the white men was a vivid tracery of leaping flames, of dry-brown bushes turning red, then disintegrating in the torrid sweep of the inferno.

Horn heard a hideous cry nearby. There was a

pounding of hoofs. Two Indian ponies staggered through the flames, seared and blackened by fire, their naked riders already ravaged and dying. There was no need to thumb a bullet at them. Horn's levelled gun sagged in his hand. Slowly he lowered his arm to his side. The fire was doing its work. There would be no other Sioux getting through. He was sure of that.

Suddenly, above the roar of the flames a new, heartening sound was heard. The peal of a bugle, the rattle of gunfire. Horn signalled to the others and drew back.

"Do you hear that shooting?" Horn asked.

"Sure thing," said Haggard. "Macy has started his own party down in the canyon. Think he'll break out?"

"Let's go and see."

They holstered their guns and trotted down the yonder slope. Brush and rocks impeded their progress. Once or twice they stumbled and fell. But now their eagerness carried them on.

A hundred yards they travelled. Two hundred yards. Five hundred yards. A half mile. Then the ground flattened out. Horn swung around a great shoulder of rock. The sound of yelling and gunfire was sharp and pronounced.

Suddenly they came within sight of the canyon, of the wide stretch of flats beyond it. Blue-clad troops were galloping out of the defile, carbines cracking, spreading out and pushing into the band of Sioux left there to prevent just such a manœuvre.

But the Sioux, split up into four separate units, were no match for Macy's cavalry. The small band in front of the troops was caught in a withering volley of rifle fire. All over the flats Indians spilled from their horses, cut down by soldier bullets.

Riderless ponies sped over the plain. Some of them went skittering up the slope toward Horn and his companions. Without any command from him they each grabbed a pony and flung themselves aboard.

In a few seconds they were in the thick of the fray, revolvers flaming in their fists. A painted Sioux spurred his pinto pony toward Horn. A knife glittered in the savage's hand. The Indian's brown arm lifted up and down in a glittering arc. Horn dodged, bending low over his pony. He felt the knife blade slice through the cloth of his shirt and nick the flesh on his back. Then he was twisting around, catching the Indian in the sights of his revolver and dropping hammer on a shot.

The pinto raced on, cutting across the path of Horn's pony. But now the pinto was riderless. The Sioux warrior had gone down in the dust.

Back and forth across the flats the battle flared. The Indians were being decimated by the vicious attack. And by the time Wild Horse and the rest of his band from the opposite cliff could join in the fight the first group had been literally wiped out.

Macy rallied his men to meet the new threat. Encouraged by the devastating success of the brush fire, which had shattered one wing of the Sioux forces and also by the swift success of their own sortie out of the boulder field, the troopers wheeled with terrible fury toward the Indians approaching from the bluff.

The cavalry split up and formed two crescents that rode around the charging Indians, pinching them in a deadly crossfire. Guns roared. Muzzle flame licked across the grey blackness of early dawn.

The Sioux rode like avenging furies, bent low over their ponies, firing at will. Troopers fell here and there. But other troopers always took their place. And the army carbines would not be denied. The Indian ranks kept thinning. Wild Horse, seeing that he was beaten, tried to gather his forces and gallop toward the canyon where a score or more of his braves were already fleeing after an unsuccessful assault from the rear.

The strength of the Indian attack in that one sector drove a wedge through the cavalry ranks. Two dozen Sioux got into the clear. Wild Horse, with another hard-riding group, hit that opening. But Horn, coming up from the middle of the line with Haggard and a score of men from Company G, closed the gap.

Two cavalrymen went down under Sioux lead, but the rest of the line held. And it was Horn who pressed his horse toward Wild Horse, angling in front of Haggard just as the Sioux chieftain fired a round at the lieutenant. The bullet screamed past Horn's head. Then, before Wild Horse could swing his carbine up for another shot, Horn drilled him through the heart.

The Sioux chieftain's mahogany-coloured face took on a greenish tinge of shock and pain. Then he sagged forward against his pony's mane. His groping fingers fastened in the pony's long dark hair for an instant. Afterwards the strength went out of his grip. His fingers opened wide and he slid lifelessly off the animal's back.

Though their leader was dead the Sioux warriors would not surrender. Wicked hand-to-hand fighting was going on all over the glade. Sabres glittered in the first rays of sunlight, slashing against knives and tomahawks.

Suddenly the last Indian was down and the battle was over. About a hundred Indians in all had escaped the trap. They were widely scattered and Macy let them go. The Sioux ponies were fresh. The cavalry mounts, on the other hand, had been ridden hard for days without proper forage.

Temporarily at least, the Sioux Nation had been smashed. Wild Horse was dead. His lodges were decimated and scattered. It would take many months for the tattered remnants to reinforce themselves and make any further trouble for the white men.

Lieutenant Haggard, his cheek bleeding from a knife slash, rode over to Horn. They were both covered with grey alkali. Black rings of weariness formed deep pools of shadow beneath their eyes.

"We did it!" Haggard murmured with an exultant ring in his voice.

Horn nodded and gave him a meagre smile. Everywhere he looked he saw the sprawled, twisted shapes of Indians. And there were many blue-clad troopers who would never swing their sabres again.

Far off to one side of the plain Horn noticed General Macy. The general signalled to them. They neck-reined their mounts and cantered over.

"Gentlemen," Macy said, "the Sioux are licked. We'll have no more trouble from them this season—thanks to that fire you and your men started on the bluff."

"It was the only way," said Horn. "They had us hemmed in and could have finished us at their leisure."

Macy nodded, his face sombre with the memory of their hazardous position the night before.

"That fire," he said musingly, "finished every Sioux up on the bluff. To us down below it looked like the whole mesa was ablaze. There were only two things they could do. Stay there and be cremated or jump and die on the rocks at the bottom of the canyon. Most of them jumped."

Horn listened in sombre silence. He felt no pleasure in what he had done. The issue had been clear-cut. Either Macy's troopers died or the Sioux died. There had been no alternative—no middle course. Yet, the thought of the terrible carnage the fire must have wrought filled him with a strange sadness. It was a sadness rooted in a deep-seated regret that white men found it necessary to engage in unceasing war upon the redmen. This war—this battle against Wild Horse and his Sioux—was as senseless as the bitter war that had been raging these many months between the armies of the North and the South.

And yet, somehow out of these wars, from these hideous deaths and agonies, must come a new peace, a new hope for the future of the country. All this was but another trial by fire for a nation still young, still struggling for its place in the sun. In their own peculiar fashion the Revolution and the War of 1812 had been trials by fire. After each of those conflicts America had emerged stronger and greater than ever before.

Perhaps some day men would say the same about the war of rebellion. But now with the smoke and dust of battle still in the air and the vision of death all around him, Horn thought of the men in butternut grey and navy blue who were slaughtering each other in the fields of Virginia and Tennessee and he was not at all sure what the end would be.

Then the thought of Kay and the missing steamboat drove all other considerations from Horn's mind. His mouth tightened and he said with quick concern:

"General, I'd like your permission to take a detail to the river to see if I can locate *The Queen*. I'm worried about our supplies—and about Kay Graham."

Macy frowned. He tugged at the lobe of his right ear.

"Wait," he said. "Will a detail be enough? How do you know there aren't more Sioux in front of us? I'd forgotten all about the packet. I wonder if Wild Horse could have attacked *The Queen* first before hitting us."

"I've thought of that," said Horn, breathing hard. "It's quite possible. However, judging by the tracks we were following, I'd say Wild Horse's band was in front of us all the time and travelling in the same direction. They wouldn't have had much time to attack the packet and still be ready to set that trap for us."

"It may have been another band of Sioux," Macy pointed out.

"That's true," Horn agreed. His face was white. The memory of Kay was very real, very compelling to his senses. If anything happened to her . . . He caught his breath as a sick fear churned his

248

insides. He added through stiff lips: "In any event, I mean to find out."

"Go ahead," said Macy, "Take a hundred men. If you spot more Sioux don't start any action. Send for help. I'll be along with the rest of the command as soon as we clean up here."

Horn changed to a saddled cavalry horse and rode off. At a signal from Macy, Haggard followed. They pushed through the mixed companies of troops and Haggard, aided by Lieutenant Lowell, told off a hundred men. There was no ceremony about it. Lowell called out a bunch of names, gestured peremptorily to men from other companies he did not know.

Within five minutes the detail, dusty, and weary and ragged, sped toward the Yellowstone several miles away.

Chapter 20

A swift rush of air slapped against their faces as Kay and Irene plunged from *The Queen*'s rail. Then the muddy Yellowstone closed over them. Locked in a desperate embrace, they were dragged all the way to the bottom of the turgid current.

Pressure beat against their lungs and Kay thought they would never rise again to the surface. Irene's clinging body was a squirming weight in her arms. At last, with a powerful thrust of her legs, Kay surfaced, pulling Irene with her. Kay drew fresh air into her tortured lungs while Irene frantically flailed the water with her palms.

Irene's senseless splashing spun her away from Kay. Immediately she began to sink. Kay made a dive for her, caught her under the armpits, and hauled her clear again.

"Turn over on your back!" Kay ordered. "Hurry!" Her own breathing was laboured and irregular.

Irene did not answer. She was too far gone in panic to do anything but fling herself upon Kay. She got one arm around Kay's neck. Her sharp fingernails raked Kay's throat. They started to go under. Kay felt the first warning of weariness gripping her muscles. In desperation she swung her closed fist against Irene's jaw.

The blow jolted Irene, snapped her eyes shut. She went limp. Kay swam near, turned Irene over on her back. Then she slid one arm across Irene's chest and began the long pull toward shore.

She risked a brief glance toward the steaming packet. She saw three men leap into the river from the freight deck. Then another long-limbed figure catapulted into the water from the promenade.

Flames, surrounded by a dark pall of smoke, poured out of the windows of Kay's cabin. Seconds later the door dissolved in a crackling roar.

Then a sudden hush descended. It was followed at once by a deep, shuddering crash. The concussion slammed heavily against Kay's eardrums. The entire port side of *The Queen* blew outward and upward. The big sternwheeler folded in the middle. A great wall of fire flickered in the mangled sections of timber. Up and up in a quivering red ladder the flames rose, gnawing hungrily through the dry wood.

A cloud of smashed debris littered the twilight sky. Jagged timber ends, sections of railing, a blackened piece of metal from a chimney, were limned against a bank of red-tinged clouds before they slowly tumbled into the river.

The two shattered sections of the packet were completely obliterated by fire as they sank beneath the rolling brown surface of the Yellowstone.

Nearer the shore, Kay still struggled through the water, pulling Irene with her. Her right arm was growing numb now and there wasn't much power in her stroke.

The twilight deepened. Along the river bank the willows were already shadowed and dark. Kay angled her course toward the nearest tree. Suddenly her knee scraped the muddy bottom. She stopped swimming, stumbled to her feet. Then she bent down, caught Irene under the armpits and dragged her up on the low bank. Kay sank down beside Irene, reaching for air. She could feel the pounding of her heart beneath her ribs. There was a chill in the air. She shivered. Her dress clung wetly to her flesh.

She pushed her tangled hair out of her eyes, then bent down beside Irene who now opened her eyes and stirred restlessly.

Kay whispered, "Are you all right, Irene?"

Irene watched her bewilderedly. "How did I get here?"

"By swimming."

"But I—I can't swim," Irene whispered in protest. Slowly her fingers caressed a lump on the side of her chin.

Kay said quickly, "That lump is from my fist. I had to hit you to keep you from dragging us both under the water."

There was a pause. Irene's head rolled from side to side. Through the gathering gloom her cheeks held a strange luminosity.

"I—I'm sorry," she whispered. "You should have let me go."

"Don't be silly." Kay moved closer. "Better turn over and get on your knees. You swallowed a good deal of water. Put your head down low."

Kay helped the other girl. For a little while Irene was sick. Afterward she fell back on the grass and rested. Darkness slid through the trees, drawing a cool black blanket around them.

They were aroused by a crashing sound in the trees some distance upriver. Kay got up quickly.

252

"What is it, Kay?" Irene asked tensely. She was fully dependent on Kay now.

"Somebody is coming this way," Kay whispered. "Might be some of those Sioux braves who were waiting for our friend Wade. Come on. Back in the water we go."

"No, Kay."

"What do you think will happen if those Sioux get their hands on us? Just use your imagination."

Kay kept her voice low, but there was a crisp, warning ring to her words. Irene offered no further objections. Kay assisted her to her feet, then led her down to the river's edge. They slid into the water, wading carefully downstream until they reached a clump of overhanging willows. They sank down in the water keeping only their heads above the surface and waited in shivering silence.

The night was thoroughly cool now and the current of the Yellowstone added its own distinct chill to their discomfort. Then, after a short interval, they saw a gleam of light moving through the trees close to the river's edge.

The moving light soon became a blazing pine knot held in the hand of a bearded man wearing the uniform of a U.S. cavalryman.

"Soldiers," said Irene and she started to rise.

Kay clamped a hand on her mouth and pushed her down so roughly that the other girl was almost completely submerged.

"They're Wade's Jayhawkers," she whispered. "Be still."

The man with the torch came on steadily. His head was cast down and his eyes scanned the grass ahead of him. More brush crackled behind him. Other men pushed into view.

"Jack," said the man with the torch, "I tell you it's no use. Those two buckos are at the bottom of the Yellowstone."

"I don't think so," said a man searching on his left. Kay recognised Wade's sharp, incisive voice. Wade went on gruffly. "Kay Graham can swim and she's got plenty of sand. I saw her heading for shore and she was dragging the other girl with her."

"Yeah, that was when we jumped off the packet. Both girls were in midstream then. It was a long haul to shore." The man with the torch turned around to scan their back trail. "I don't like it. We should be getting out of here. Those damned redskins aren't going to relish losing those rifles we promised them."

Wade, his head lowered as he crouched to study the grass along the bank, spoke over his shoulder.

"How do you think I like it? That damned Graham girl made me lose a fortune. I'd like to settle with her."

"What would you do if you found her?" the other man asked. There was a sly, eager curiosity in his question.

"Figure that one out yourself," snapped Wade. "But I'd make her pay and pay for every rifle that went down with that packet."

Kay felt numb with cold. She had to clamp her teeth together to keep them from chattering. Wade and his men were coming closer. She wondered if they would venture close to the bank where she and Irene had lain after first leaving the river. The signs there would be unmistakable.

"They must be around here somewhere," raged Wade. "They couldn't have gone far."

There was a faint, far-off sound back in the brush. Again the man with the torch whirled around. His face, close to the leaping glare of the flames, was larded with nervous sweat. Fear muddied his eyes.

"Jack," he said, "we've got to clear out. Those Indians are coming this way. We lost six men in that explosion. There are only six of us left."

"Don't get boogery."

The muffled sound of hoofbeats was telegraphed to their ears by the night wind. Branches crackled somewhere ahead. "All right," hissed Wade. "Douse that torch."

The man with the torch hurled the pine knot into the dirt and quickly stamped out the flames. For a moment, then, Kay watching this scene from the willows, lost them in the darkness. But her eyes quickly became adjusted to the darkness and she realized that a pale light filtered down through the trees from a sky now filled with stars.

Wade and his companions huddled together in a compact group, looking toward their back trail.

"We'll cut inland," he said, "and try to sneak around them. If Wild Horse was sticking to his bargain to supply us with horses to reach Fort Union, maybe we can steal the critters from the Indian camp while they're scouring the brush for us."

"Suppose the horses are guarded?" one of the men asked.

"Hell, we fight for them, then," said Wade. "We can't last long in this country without horses. Besides, the rest of the crew will be waiting for us around Fort Union after decoying those infantry soldiers away from *The Queen*. If we can nab horses now we'll be in Fort Union in two days. Then we'll see about stealing one of those supply packets to get us to Fort Benton."

Wade's voice faded out as he nudged his men into movement. They stole through the trees, angling away from the Yellowstone. After a moment the sound of their departure was completely absorbed by the rapid *clop-clop* of hoofs. A column of naked Sioux warriors rode into the little clearing. They stopped near the spot where Wade and his men had discussed their plans. One brave dismounted, found the charred pine faggot. He spoke a few guttural words to the other Indian riders. Then he quickly flung himself

256

aboard his pony and the entire band went crashing through the trees on the trail of Wade's group.

Kay and Irene, shivering with cold in the shallow water of the Yellowstone, waited for all sounds to dissolve in the darkness before they ventured up on the bank again. Their dresses felt cold and clammy against their bodies. Hunger, too, began to add its nagging appeal to their increasing discomfort.

"We've got to make a fire and get our clothes off," said Kay, her arm around Irene.

"Not here, Kay," said Irene, shaking with cold. "The Indians would see it at once."

"I know. We've got to move on. Downriver toward Glendive. Walking will help the blood to circulate. And after we get far enough away from here maybe we can risk a fire."

She started off through the trees. Irene held back.

"I'm tired, Kay. I can't walk."

Kay's reply was savagely impatient. "I'm just as tired as you. But if you want to live much longer you'll walk. We're not too far from Glendive. If Macy's troops get through we might meet them."

"But you heard what Wade said about that. They haven't a chance."

"Irene, you never saw the cavalry fight. I'm betting on them."

She pulled Irene roughly after her through the trees. They followed the course of the river, stumbling over rocks and steep grass hummocks. It was painfully slow going. Twice Kay had to pull Irene to her feet after the latter had fallen.

They had traversed a half mile when the sound of shooting broke out far to the rear.

"That's Wade making his bid for those Sioux ponies," Kay said and plodded on without pausing.

They walked for the better part of two hours. By that time Kay's feet were sore and every bone in her body ached with weariness. Irene was almost completely done in. For the last half mile Kay had to support her, literally drag her forward.

Finally Irene slipped to the ground and refused to rise.

"You go on, Kay," she gasped. "I can't walk any more." When Kay bent toward her as if she were about to haul her to her feet, she pleaded: "Please, I can't."

Kay nodded and said wearily, "All right."

They had come around the base of a small bluff sheltered from the wind. Kay looked around her, saw some dry sticks and brush, and decided to risk a fire. It took a little time before she was able to start a small blaze by rubbing two sticks together. But once started, the fire spread rapidly to the pile of brush she had gathered.

The fire brought a welcome warmth to their chilled bodies. They hovered close to the flames, letting the heat dry out their clothes. It occurred to Kay that other Sioux bands might be prowling in the area, but she thrust the thought aside. They needed this fire and they needed rest more than anything else.

Although she had planned to rest for only a few hours Kay succumbed to the same overwhelming weariness that claimed Irene soon after they had the fire going. Kay fell into a deep sleep and when she woke dawn was breaking in the east. She sat up, stretching to drive the kinks out of her body. The fire was a mass of blackened ashes. Irene was still asleep, her face pale and worn, yet somehow sweet in repose.

Kay went over and roused the other girl. She saw at once that Irene had been thoroughly used up by the events of the previous night. She experienced her moment of doubt, then, as to how Irene would endure the rigours that lay inevitably ahead of them—the heat and the hunger, the thirst and the weariness of more walking.

It took considerable persuasion to get Irene back on her feet. She begged Kay to go without her. There was no spirit left in her. She was completely done up. And Kay, fully understanding that her strength would have to sustain them both, pulled her up.

They travelled slowly—Irene's fatigue dictated the pace—through a morning already bright with the promise of heat. The ground along the river was rough and uneven. Clinging vines, numerous deadfalls, and low hummocks of grass blocked their way time and again, forcing them to make wide detours away from the Yellowstone.

Hunger nagged unceasingly at them, for they had not eaten in twenty-four hours. But Kay kept on, fighting against the poison of fatigue that grew within her.

An hour before noon, with Irene complaining that she could not walk another step, they found an Indian canoe concealed in some bushes.

"This is the break we need," said Kay. An eager light animated her tired features.

She pushed the canoe into the water, helped Irene into the narrow seat in the prow. Irene sat there limply, thin hands gripping the sides.

"You'll have to paddle, Kay," she said.

"I'd already planned on that," Kay replied.

She picked up the crude Indian paddle, sculled the light craft out into midstream, then headed downriver toward Glendive.

The sun skidded high into the brassy blue sky. Heat ravished the earth. It shimmered in dancing waves above the glistening water. Kay felt the burn of the sun's rays on her cheeks. It was like the sting of a hundred tiny needles, pricking her flesh.

The canoe, aided by the down-sweeping current, made rapid progress. In the prow Irene slumped in a half sleep, too weak now to sit up. Kay, too, felt the moving tide of exhaustion in her. Yet, she would not give in to her weakness. The hardness and stubbornness that were so much a part of her nature came through to triumph over her weariness.

Her motions were mechanical. The paddle dipped in and out of the muddy water with a monotonous regularity. Each stroke shot the canoe forward on the crest of the choppy current.

Noon went by. Then one o'clock and two. An hour later the light Indian craft slid out of the black shadow of a high bluff into blinding sunlight. There was a shout far ahead along the shore. Kay's head came up. The paddle lifted from the river. Water dripped from the smooth blade. The canoe drifted downriver.

Again the shout reached her ears. Kay blinked her eyes, trying to peer through the blinding blaze of heat. Then she caught a sign of movement among the trees several hundred yards away. A troop of cavalry galloped into view. The lead riders lifted their hands in salute. Dust rose up in a billowing cloud as the troopers bent low and urged their mounts forward at a faster gait.

"Irene!" called Kay. "There's the cavalry!"

The other girl straightened. A faint cry spilled from her lips. She turned around toward Kay and tears started from her flickering eyelids. She strained forward, almost tipping the canoe. Harsh, high-pitched laughter rolled from her until Kay yelled to her to stop.

The cavalry sped along the river bank. A cheer

rippled up and down the ranks as Kay waved back and deftly swung the canoe toward shore. The light craft ground into the mud, came to a shivering halt. Irene rose, waited for Kay to approach. Kay jumped to the ground, gave her hand to Irene, helped the other girl down beside her.

The blue-clad troopers came on with a rush. Hoofs beat the earth in a solid drum-roll of sound. Kay saw Bill Horn at the head of the column. She forgot Irene. She forgot all about the hostility and anger that had gripped her when they'd last said good-bye two weeks ago. She forgot the scene on the deck of the *Western Star* when the sight of Irene emerging from Horn's cabin with a nightgown on her arm had driven her ashore in a fuming, jealous rage.

There was no room for anything in her mind and heart but the sight of Horn leaving the saddle of his horse and rushing toward her with the sound of her name on his lips. She saw the hard break of feeling in his mobile face. Then she was lost in his arms.

He kissed her, and it was as if no one had ever kissed her before. She felt the fierce pressure of his arms holding her against him. His mouth, too, was bruising hers. But there was an ecstatic sweetness in the pain, and her lips gave back all the warmth and tumult that came from him.

Horn was breathing hard when he released her. She leaned against him. She looked up at him.

At this moment she was completely feminine—a woman lovely and desirable, with love's magic in her eyes and in the smiling curve of her lips.

"Damn it, Kay," Horn said gruffly. "You gave me a scare. I thought you—that I—I'd seen the last of you." He paused blushing under his dark stubble of beard. "Kay—about that afternoon in front of my cabin when Irene . . . it wasn't like you thought . . ."

She smiled and said in quick contrition, "I know . . . I know. I—I was a fool. I—I just couldn't help it." She pressed her face against him.

"Are you all right?" he asked.

"Yes," she said, drawing slightly away to look at him. "There's only one thing. I'm hungry."

"When did you eat last?"

"Yesterday at noon."

"Good Lord!" he said. "I'll get you something." He paused as if he had suddenly remembered something. "The entire command has been on short rations for the last two days. We were counting on *The Queen* to stock up. Tell me, Kay. What happened?"

"Wait," she said. "I'm forgetting all about Irene."

She swung around, Horn at her side. A short distance away Irene was surrounded by a group of solicitous troopers.

"Irene seems to be doing all right for herself," Horn observed.

"It was pretty tough for her," Kay said.

"Tough for you, too, Kay."

Irene was walking slowly toward them now. One lanky trooper had a big hand tucked under her elbow. She smiled wanly at Horn and extended her slim fingers. Horn gripped them.

"Hello, Bill," she said.

This was a subdued, soberly sincere Irene. She was no longer playing her sly woman's game with him. He saw, too, that immediate warmth showed in her glance when she looked at Kay.

"I'm glad you're all right," Horn said.

"Yes," Irene answered. "Thanks to Kay. She made me do a lot of things I didn't think I could do. That's the only reason I'm here."

Kay blushed at this unstinted praise and Irene added with sudden heat, "It's true, Kay, and don't you deny it." She looked around at the rest of the members of the detail, then asked: "Where is Lieutenant Breadon? I don't see him here."

"He was wounded in the fight with Wild Horse and his Sioux," Horn told her.

Immediate concern showed in her face. "Is he—will he be all right?"

"He's going to pull through, Irene."

Horn signalled to Trooper Freon who had accompanied the detail.

"Freon, do you have any food in your saddle bags?"

"Yes, sir. A little dried jerky and some biscuits."

"Will you please give some to Miss Graham and Miss Nostrum?"

Trooper Arley and a few others came over to add their meagre rations to that supplied by Freon. And there were even a few swallows of water left in Arley's canteen to wash down the dry tasteless food.

As Kay munched gratefully on a biscuit Horn hunkered down beside her on the grass.

"Now let's have the story of what happened to you and your packet, Kay," he urged.

"We were tricked by Jack Wade and a bunch of his Jayhawkers," she said simply.

"Wade?" he repeated, his features clouding up. "Then it wasn't the Sioux?"

"No. It happened two days ago near sunset. The crew was out cutting wood for the boilers. Half of the infantry detail went along as guards. Then we heard the sound of gunfire off in the woods. It grew heavier. Finally Sergeant Temple decided to take the rest of the troops to reinforce Captain Sumner's men.

"While they were gone Wade and his men surprised us. They were dressed in U.S. cavalry uniforms and they were aboard before we realized who they were. Tug Willison was killed. Wade took *The Queen* upriver. It seems this was all part of a plan. A small group of Sioux were to meet him at the junction of the Yellowstone and the Tongue. Wade was to hand over all the rifles and ammunition on board in return for a lot of furs and some Indian ponies."

As Kay paused to take a sip of water from Trooper Arley's canteen Horn gave expression to his feelings.

"I've got a long, full account to settle with Wade. I hope the chance comes soon. But how did you get away? And where is Wade now?"

Kay's face was grim when she answered.

"I made up my mind I'd rather lose *The Queen* than see the Sioux get the guns and supplies we were carrying. So I waited for a chance to set fire to the boat." She went on to explain the ruse she had played on Wade, enabling her to disarm him and forcing him to stand idly by while she started the blaze in her cabin. "There was a box of dynamite in the cabin," she concluded. "You can guess how high *The Queen* blew when the flames hit that giant powder."

"All of which meant no rifles for the Sioux," Irene added, as she proceeded to outline the rest of their experiences.

When Irene had finished Horn looked with unconcealed admiration at Kay. She had deliberately risked her life and destroyed one of the best packets in the Missouri River trade for the sake of the safety of Macy's expedition. The loss might ruin her business. But it was obvious from her unruffled manner that she was giving it no consideration.

"You cut things mighty fine," he said at last.

"There was no other way," she answered simply. "Wade let us know that General Macy's command was riding into a trap and that Wild Horse planned to rally some other bands to his side, then use *The Queen*'s supplies in an attempt to sack Fort Union. I knew then that *The Queen* had to be destroyed."

"It was a wonderful sacrifice to make, Kay," Horn said. "You've helped more than any of us will ever know."

"But how about you?" Kay asked. "You must have avoided the trap Wade was talking about."

"No, we rode right into it. But we fought our way out. They had us surrounded in a rocky glade with a bunch of warriors on two bluffs in position to slaughter us. But a brush fire on top of one of the cliffs took care of one group. Then we made a rush and got out into the open and licked them."

He gave Kay a meagre description of the action, but it was enough to tell her that the entire command had come within an eyelash of being completely wiped out. And a defeat of Macy's troops could easily have meant the abandoning of Fort Union to the redmen.

"Wild Horse is dead," concluded Horn, "and I don't think the Sioux remnants will give us much trouble for the rest of the year. Macy can take his command back to the fort and wait for further orders."

"There's one more job," Kay pointed out. "The Jayhawkers that surprised *The Queen*'s wood crew were supposed to march back to Fort Union and wait for the rest of Wade's men."

"What for?" Horn demanded.

"Wade means to go to Fort Benton. The place is supposed to be swarming with gold-heavy miners from Bannock."

"He figures on making a quick killing there and then clean out?"

"That's it. And the only way he can reach Fort Benton quickly is by steamboat. He figures on stealing one of the supply packets at Fort Union for that purpose."

A sudden hard care showed in the long, angular line of Horn's jaw. He knotted the fingers of his right hand, sent them smashing into the palm of his left hand.

"The scheme is just bold enough to succeed," he said. "At night and with his men wearing cavalry uniforms he might get away with it."

Kay laid a hand upon his arm and stared up into his face. "What are you going to do?"

"I'm going to stop him," he said savagely, "if I have to follow him all the way to Fort Benton."

Chapter 21

General Macy and the main command were camped near Glendive Creek when Bill Horn and his special detail returned downriver near dusk. The general greeted Kay and Irene warmly. The story of their escape from Wade's Jayhawkers and the subsequent demolition of *The Queen* brought a look of worry to Macy's sun-scorched features.

"You did a marvellous thing, Kay," he said, "but it sure leaves my command in a spot for supplies. We're low on food and the horses need a good rest. Yet, the longer we stay here without supplementing our supplies the more dangerous our position will be."

"Did you see any signs of Captain Sumner's infantry?" Kay asked.

"Yes," Macy replied. "We ran into several of their couriers about an hour ago. They lost a half-dozen men in that fight in the woods. The rest of the time they spent trekking upriver trying to find *The Queen*. Sumner has a detail somewhere south and west of us still hunting you two ladies."

Horn, who was standing with Lieutenant Lowell and Haggard, now stepped forward.

"General, with your permission I'd like to go after Wade," he said. There was a dark destructiveness showing in his high-boned face. "You heard what Kay said about Wade's plans."

"Do you think he'd try to steal a packet from Fort Union after what's happened?"

"I do," said Horn. "With the Sioux licked and his own force pared down and the cavalry free to roam this whole country to clean up any stray bands, it's more than ever important for Wade to clear out fast. I'd like to stop him—for personal reasons."

Macy did not answer immediately. He let his frowning glance linger on the weary men of his command. The loss of *The Queen* was strongly in his mind. It turned him morose and slightly bitter.

"I'm more concerned about the entire command," he said finally. "Wade can wait. But we need food and there's no game to be had in this area in midsummer. We're a two-day march from Fort Union—and that's with good horses."

Horn was silent and thoughtful. Then he said, "There might be a way out, General."

Macy's attention swivelled back to the riverboat captain.

"What do you suggest?"

"Give me two dozen men. Let us pick the best of the horses. We'll ride to Fort Union as fast as we can. If you think you can hold out here for a few days I'll send a steamboat up here with supplies."

Macy's ruddy face relaxed in a slow, knowing smile.

"What about Wade?" he queried.

"If the general will not need me for a few days I'd like his permission to go after Wade."

Macy looked at Horn, sensing the hard tumult that was in him.

"You have the general's permission," he said at last. "I reckon the rest of us can pull in our belts until you send that packet up here. But it had better be soon. The Yellowstone is going down fast. Two weeks from now no steamboat ever built will be able to navigate the river."

"Thanks," said Horn. "Thanks very much."

Macy nodded. "Good luck. Take the men you want."

Because Horn was anxious to start as soon as possible he lost no time in asking for volunteers. More than two-score troopers answered the call. Since General Macy had assigned Lieutenant Haggard to the special detail, Horn left the actual task of choosing men to Haggard.

In twenty minutes the small column of cavalry was ready. The troopers flung themselves into their saddles, waited for the signal to ride. It was then that Kay walked to the edge of camp and stopped Horn.

"Bill, can you use another rider?" she asked.

Horn shifted in the saddle, looking down at her,

feeling now, as always, the strong thrust of desire in him whenever he was near her.

"Sorry, Kay," he said. "This promises to be a tough grind. What follows with Wade may be even more unpleasant."

She smiled at him. There was tenderness in her eyes—a warm regard meant only for him. But there was a hint of stubborn will in her next words.

"I have a stake in this game, too, Bill," she reminded him.

Horn thought of the destroyed packet, of Kay's part in the entire campaign, and understood how right she was. He swung out of the saddle to stand beside her.

"Better for you to stay here, Kay. You've been through enough trouble in the last few days. I don't want you to take any more chances."

Rebellion showed in her deep blue eyes. But she surprised Horn by nodding her acquiescence. They remained there close together. Horn felt the solid beat of his pulses. He wanted to pull her into his arms and he thought that she was waiting for him to do just that. Then a trooper coughed nearby and he was reminded of the others. So he smiled at her and stepped to his horse.

Kay drew back, returning his smile, her mouth softly curved and just faintly amused. She heard Horn yell, "Let's go," and watched the small group of riders gallop off through the trees.

With a fifteen-minute rest stop every hour Horn was able to pace the horses steadily through the first half of the night. Near twelve o'clock they finally made camp close to the Yellowstone and staked the tired horses out to graze.

At dawn they were up again and ready to continue their journey. They had eaten some dry biscuits and washed them down with water secured from a convenient spring and were cinching down their saddles when the sound of a running horse reached them.

Without any signal from Haggard or Horn, the men deployed through the trees, carbines at the ready. The horse came steadily on and it was Horn who caught the first glimpse of Kay Graham.

She was riding a big black gelding. It was obvious at a glance that she knew how to handle horses. She rode well and with a minimum of effort. She came on with her hair flying in the breeze, her blue eyes clear and alert. The gelding skidded to a halt close to Horn.

"I wondered if I'd be coming to your camp soon," she said with a sly amusement shining in her eyes.

An astonished murmur ran through the soldiers in the detail as they lowered their carbines and slowly wandered back to their mounts. Haggard joined Horn and politely removed his forage cap.

"Good morning, Lieutenant," she greeted him.

"Good morning, Miss Graham," he answered, his eyes warmly and gently regarding her.

"Kay," said Horn, frowning despite the pleasure he felt at having her near again, "you shouldn't have come."

"Bill is right," added Haggard. "This trip is not for a woman—if you'll pardon my saying so."

"But now that I'm here . . ." She didn't finish. She looked down at Horn, seeing how troubled he was, how determined he was to get on with the grim business that lay ahead.

"I reckon you'll have to stick with us, Kay," Horn said. "But you'll have to keep up."

"Don't worry," she assured him. "I've ridden horses since I was a kid in pigtails. You won't lose me."

"But what about Macy?" Haggard asked, his manner worried.

"I sneaked away after the camp had quieted down," Kay said. "And I left a note for Irene, telling her where I was going and that I could take care of myself."

"I reckon you can at that," the lieutenant agreed. "You've been doing a man's job in a man's war so far. I suppose you've got a right to go on doing it."

"That's exactly how I feel," she said and watched Horn as she spoke.

His features showed no change for a moment. The skin was drawn tight over his cheekbones and his eyes were dark and deep with the sombre run of his thinking. Finally he nodded and gave her the edge of a grim smile. It was a meagre gesture. But she expected no more, for she understood the wildness that was in him now, the hard recklessness that drove all considerations from his mind except coming to grips with Wade.

He had no room for her at this time. He had a job to do and he meant to do it—if it was not already too late. It was this singleness of purpose, this driving will, that made him so dangerous and so capable. And it was a quality she thoroughly appreciated in him.

And so she felt no resentment when he offered no further comment, but turned and stepped into the saddle.

They rode all of that day, made a dry camp a little after dark and continued on again at four in the morning, arriving at the Missouri River shore opposite Fort Union three hours later. Men and horses were thoroughly used up by that time. Yet, one man among them—Bill Horn—remained strong and tensely eager. There was a tough fibre in him that would not yield to weariness.

The soldier guard along the opposite landing spotted them and an immediate shout went up. A courier was sent back to the fort and from the pilothouse of the *Western Star* moored to the landing the head and shoulders of a man appeared. He sent a ringing yell across the river.

Horn recognized Dave London and shouted back.

"Get up some steam," Horn yelled, cupping his hands around his mouth, "and ferry us over."

Smoke was already gently puffing from the *Western Star*'s chimneys. Now, as Dave London withdrew inside the pilothouse, the smoke increased in volume, turning darker and heavier. Bells began to ring inside the packet.

In a little while the steamboat chuffed across the Missouri. The landing stage was run down and the detail came aboard. Then the packet turned about and steamed back to the other side. During the short ride Horn had time to notice that there was only one other packet tied up at the landing and he wondered if Wade had made his appearance.

He got his answer when Dave London came running across the freight deck to greet him with a hardy slap on the back.

"Bill, it's good to see you," he said. "I thought maybe by this time you were a scalp dangling from a Sioux Indian's belt."

"There was a time when none of us were very far from it," Horn told him. Then, going straight to the heart of his mission, he asked: "Dave, have Jack Wade and his renegades been here?"

"Yeah. How did you know?"

"Never mind. Did they get away with one of the supply packets?"

London nodded, amazed. "They sure did, the

damned sidewinders. It happened a couple of hours before dawn. Those blue uniforms fooled the soldier guard. By the time the troops realized the trick it was too late. Four of them were killed."

Horn's lips moved in silent rage. When he did speak his words were heavy and weighted with the fury of his determination.

"Just a little too late," he said. "I was afraid of that. But the game isn't over yet."

"You mean you're going after him?" London demanded eagerly.

"Yes, Dave," Horn said with quiet deadliness, "and this time I'll get him. What boat did he take?"

"The *Silas Hardy*, a small supply steamer."

"I know it. No match for the *Western Star*."

"But what happened with Macy's command?" asked London. "And how did you know about Wade? Was he in that ruckus with the Sioux?"

With sharp and savage precision Horn sketched for London a bare outline of the events that had occurred since General Macy's regiment of cavalry had marched out of Fort Union.

"Man alive!" said London when he had finished. "I'd have given my right arm to be along. Sounds even better than Shiloh and Pittsburg Landing. When are you planning to go after Wade?"

"Just as soon as I report to Captain Bevens at the fort and relay General Macy's orders about a relief packet for the rest of the command."

Chapter 22

At ten o'clock the next morning the *Western Star* steamed past Big Muddy Creek which came in at a sharp tangent from the north. And still there was no sign of the stolen packet.

The *Western Star* was throbbing in every joint as the solid beat of the pounding pistons shook the river boat from stem to stern. A flat iron had been hung on the safety valve down in the engine room in order to squeeze every ounce of pressure out of the seething boilers.

All night, without stopping, the *Western Star* had pushed its pointed prow through the muddy current of the Missouri. And up in the pilothouse Bill Horn clung to the wheel, refusing all offers, both from Dave London and from Kay Graham, to be relieved.

At first, Horn had tried to persuade Kay to take over the job of piloting the relief packet up the Yellowstone. But Kay had been insistent in her determination to go along with the *Western Star.*

Now, as Horn strained his weary eyes to peer ahead through the shimmering heat haze that cloaked the Missouri, he heard the pilothouse door flung open behind him.

"Bill!" It was Dave London and he was out of breath after his climb from the lower decks. "We're getting low on cordwood. We'll soon have to stop and cut some timber."

Horn jerked his head around, still maintaining his hold upon the wheel spokes. "No time to stop now, Dave. How long can we go on what's left?"

"Half an hour. That's all."

"All right," Horn snapped. "When the wood is used up start breaking up the furniture in the cabins."

"You don't mean that you—"

"I mean I don't intend to stop the *Western Star* until I've used up every stick of wood on this packet," Horn cut in grimly.

"But if they've sailed all night just as we have they could still be miles ahead," London protested.

Horn stared out through the glass windows, but his voice reached London and Kay, standing a few feet away, with distinct clearness. And it carried a solid ring of conviction.

"I checked with the soldier guards at the fort, Dave. That packet Wade took carried only a small load of wood. If they travelled all night I'll wager they've already had to make one or two stops to cut wood. That's what'll beat them." His voice lifted a notch and the knuckles of his powerful hands grew white and hard around the wheel spokes. "Tell Lieutenant Haggard to get his troopers ready for action."

London stood by the door, watching Horn. Slowly he shook his head. He was never more conscious of the tremendous energy, the unceasing drive, of this man who had been his companion on the Missouri for many years. It was a compelling thing and it turned London silently away.

When he had gone Kay came over to Horn. She stood beside him, watching the muddy swirl of current that divided before the jutting prow of the steamboat, skimmed choppily past the sides, then reunited in a smother of yellow foam, at the stern.

"Let me take over, Bill," Kay urged gently. "You're tired. You've been standing at the wheel all night."

He glanced down at her. For just a moment the hard planes of his face relaxed. The shadow of a smile lifted the corners of his mouth. Then the bleakness, the hardness, came back.

"Not now, Kay," he said. "It won't be long."

She looked at him with a close attention. "You think we'll catch up to Wade soon?"

"Yes. I'm sure of it."

It was a rippling pressure in his shoulders, a feeling that would not be denied. Excitement began to hammer in his veins.

Five minutes passed. Ten minutes. Kay said

nothing. She stood beside Horn, watching the river unwind before them. Then, as they were gliding through the final bend of an S loop, they sighted the *Silas Hardy.*

"There it is!" Kay cried.

Horn nodded and mechanically rang the engine room for more speed. The *Western Star* ploughed steadily on. At last the other boat vanished around the curve. But in a few minutes the *Western Star* steamed past the bend and there was the *Silas Hardy,* just a thousand yards away.

A strident shout rose from the freight deck. Boots pounded on the companionway. Dave London burst into the room.

"Bill, you were right," he exclaimed. "We've caught them!"

Horn pointed through the window glass.

"Look at that smoke, I want more steam."

Black clouds of smoke were pouring from the stacks of the other river packet.

"Wade has seen us," Horn added. "And he's crowding every pound of steam out of those boilers." He watched the wavering column of smoke. "I reckon he's using resin or turpentine on his fires. Well, we can do the same."

"You'll blow the boat sky high," London protested.

"I'll take that chance," Horn snapped.

"But there's Kay . . ." London began and stopped.

Horn twisted around. Change stirred in his high-boned cheeks. His fingers eased their hard grip on the wheel.

Kay said quickly, "You do what you want, Bill." There was no fear, no cringe in her. "I've used turpentine myself. In this case I'd say it was worth the risk."

Her quick smile brought a rash grin to Horn's lips. He turned to London.

"Go ahead, Dave. Before they draw away from us."

London looked toward the other packet. The smoke belching from the steamboat's twin chimneys shot into the sky like tall, wavering pillars.

"They are gaining, Bill," London said. "We'll stop that."

He went out swiftly. Horn and Kay heard his clattering descent down the companionway. The other boat was slowly opening the gap between the *Western Star* and itself. Horn watched it draw away, impatiently waiting for the answering surge of power from the *Western Star*'s boilers.

At length he felt the tug of the rising steam pressure as the sweating men in the engine room began feeding turpentine and resin to the fires. The dull throbbing of the pistons filled the packet with a hammering vibration. Water swirled higher around the pointed prow of the packet as it cut faster and faster through the Missouri.

Now the *Western Star* began to gain. The columns of smoke from the other packet grew thicker as Wade pressed for every knot of speed. And still the *Western Star* gained.

A wild exultation sang in Horn's veins. This was the moment he had long been waiting for. This was the showdown between Wade and himself. It was a showdown too long deferred. This was to be the end of the trail—for one of them.

London returned and rushed to the pilothouse windows.

"We're pulling up on them, Bill," he said eagerly. Horn nodded and London added: "Haggard has his soldiers ready."

"Good." Horn turned to Kay. "Kay, when we get up close I'm going to turn the wheel over to you. I mean to be in on this scrap. The engine room crew will stay on duty to take orders from you and I'll leave a couple of deckhands below on guard while the rest of us board the other packet."

Kay said, "You'll want me to swing in alongside the other packet."

"Right. But watch out for flying lead. Keep down below that metal screen beyond the windows. When we get alongside we'll use grappling hooks to keep the boats together."

Only five hundred yards separated the packets. Still the *Western Star* gained. Now rifle fire, punctuated by puffs of blue-grey smoke, issued from the decks of the other packet. Most of the bullets fell short. But as the *Western Star* drew within range lead began to slam into the sides of the army craft.

"Time to go," said Horn and drew Kay toward the wheel. "And be careful."

"No, Bill," she murmured gently. "I say that to you." She placed both hands against his chest. She did not kiss him. She merely said, "I'll be waiting for you."

He was gone, then, striding swiftly out the door and pounding down the companionway after Dave London. Outside the rattle of guns was more distinct. Smoke obscured a portion of the deck of Wade's boat and now, from behind bales and barrels, Haggard's troopers began to return the fire of Wade's renegades. A trooper handed Horn a carbine and he dropped down behind a bale and drilled a shot toward the other packet.

Somewhere deep in the stern a trooper cried out in agony and fell lifeless to the deck. The distance between the packets had been cut to a mere hundred feet now. The firing was deadly. Bullets kept hammering into the dry wooden planks of the *Western Star*.

Half a dozen deckhands appeared behind Horn. They held long grappling hooks in their hands and big lengths of rope. The *Western Star* was swerving toward the other packet now. Wade, in turn, tried to swing away. But Kay kept crowding him.

During a lull in firing Haggard passed an order out to his troopers.

"Have your sidearms ready. I'll give the signal when we're ready to rush the other boat."

The *Western Star* ground against the other packet. There was a wicked volley of lead from Wade's men. Then came a jarring crash as the two packets came together. The impact shook the *Western Star*, made it heel far over in the current, then swing back.

"Forward!" yelled Haggard and rose from his hiding place.

With one accord the troopers rushed across the freight deck. With them ran the deckhands. One man fell, riddled by bullets. The others kept on. A grappling hook went hurtling through space to thud against the deck of Wade's packet. Another hook followed it.

There was a thunderous yell from Haggard's troopers. Colts were flaming in their hands as they leaped on to the other packet. Horn was up among the leaders. He dropped one man with a well-placed shot and moved on. Beside him Haggard and London were firing, too.

"Watch those uniforms!" Haggard yelled. "Don't shoot your own men."

This was a real danger, Horn realized, as he saw the profusion of blue uniforms around him. A bearded man charged him A gun butt grazed the side of his head and he fell to his knees.

Twisting around, he slammed a shot at the man and slid out of the way as he collapsed.

Horn got up. He edged toward the companionway. A snarling group of men, locked in a rough-and-tumble fight with knives and clubbed guns, barred his path. He hit one of the men, a stranger to him, with the barrel of his revolver and charged past.

A hurtling body hit him at the foot of the companionway. He was knocked off his feet. By the time he got up he had caught only a glimpse of a retreating back. Then as the man turned slightly he saw that it was Wade. Horn lifted his gun, then held his fire as more struggling shapes slid in front of him.

He tried to push through the mass of bales and barrels and fighting men. He had only one thought: to reach Wade. A bullet licked hotly past his face. Yonder, a Jayhawker abandoned the fight and leaped into the Missouri. One of Horn's deckhands followed, pumping lead into the water.

The sound of the *Western Star*'s whistle, caught off almost at once, drew Horn's glance to the pilothouse of his own packet. But he saw nothing out of the way. It wasn't until he found himself swept to the edge of the freight deck that he noticed the two hawsers holding the steamboats together had been severed with the blow of an axe and the boats were drifting apart.

He looked for the deckhands he had left to guard the lines. All he saw was the crumpled shape of one of the men lying near an overturned barrel. He knew, then, a sudden cold fear.

There was a faint splashing sound at the stern of the *Western Star.* The paddle wheels slowly began to churn. Horn dived into the river. It was a shallow dive that brought him quickly to the surface. The packet was sliding away from him. He levelled out in the water, swimming vigorously.

Two dozen strokes brought him to the port side of the *Western Star.* He gripped the water-soaked planking, hauled himself aboard. Struggling to his feet, he felt the deck boards shake under his palms. He glanced up and saw Garvin, one of Wade's Jayhawkers, sprinting toward him. Garvin's gun was out and spitting flame.

The first bullet droned over Horn's head. He made a frantic grab for his own revolver. He brought it up, squeezed the trigger, and heard the hammer strike, but there was no answering explosion. The water and silt from the Missouri had got into the weapon's mechanism.

Garvin fired again. Horn felt a bullet burn across his neck. Blood began to drip down to his shoulder. Crouched low, he flung his own gun at Garvin. The renegade ducked. The gun sailed past his shoulder. He was angling in for a finishing shot when Horn threw himself at his legs.

The full force of Horn's one hundred and eighty pounds struck Garvin at the knees. Garvin pitched backward, tottered momentarily as he tried to stay on his feet, then crashed heavily to the deck. The back of his head struck the planking. He stirred once, then lay still.

Horn felt the packet moving under him as he reeled toward Garvin and took the renegade's weapon. He was whirling toward the companionway when a shot from the high texas thudded into the boards at his feet. Jack Wade was up there, his face covered with a three-day growth of beard, a wicked grin plastered on his long, sensuous mouth.

"Come and get it, Bill!" Wade taunted.

Blue smoke puffed from the black maw of his gun barrel. Horn staggered as he felt a sharp jolt in his left side. He fell to one knee. Another slug droned over his head.

Pain was beginning to set up an insistent clamour along his ribs. He clamped his left hand to the wet wound and rose unsteadily.

"I'm coming, Jack," he said grimly and stumbled toward the companionway.

He heard Kay cry sharply from the texas. He looked up, ready to throw a shot at Wade, then stopped as Kay rushed at the Jayhawker. There was a reddish bruise on Kay's right cheek and her hair was mussed. Seeing that drove Horn into angry frenzy.

He ran toward the companionway. Wade followed his progress. He fired at Horn but missed when Kay flung herself at him and struck at his arm. Horn saw Wade turn and slam his fist into Kay's face.

Kay's hands flew up to her forehead. She was driven back against the wall of one of the cabins. She collapsed in a twisted heap on the deck.

Horn pumped one shot at Wade, then charged up the companionway. Blood was seeping through his shirt and the pain was now a pulsating ache. His knees were shaky. Greyness whirled before his eyes and the companionway was a long, endless tunnel stretching above him. He kept climbing and climbing and always there was another step in his way.

He gained the promenade and found Wade above him at the head of the next flight of stairs leading to the texas. Wade's gun roared. The bullet missed Horn by inches and ricocheted off the nearby railing. He ran at a low crouch to the foot of the companionway. His breathing was shallow and laboured. There was a sick, ragged roaring inside him.

He planted his right foot on the first step of the companionway. It was an effort to boost himself upward. He saw Wade, a dark blot above him, saw the down-slashing movement of Wade's gun barrel. He brought his own gun up. It was a dragging weight in his hand. It seemed he would never lift it into firing position. It was like living these seconds of his life in agonizing slow motion.

A double report banged against his ears. A ruddy lance of muzzle flame drilled toward him. His own gun bucked against his wrist. Then a slashing weight struck his hand. His fingers went numb, the weapon spilled to the steps and above him there was a sudden clatter.

He looked up through pain-glazed eyes and saw Wade's body tumbling toward him. He tried to twist away. But Wade's head and shoulders hit him squarely. They plunged down the last few steps. They hit the promenade deck, rolled over and over.

There was blood on Wade's chest and that he was hurt Horn clearly understood. But his own wounds were punishing him severely. Wade's last bullet had creased the back of Horn's right hand and it was still numb. Now Wade's left fist crashed into his jaw.

Horn took another blow in the same place, felt his senses slipping. He swung his own left fist, caught Wade under the ear.

"This is—your finish," Wade panted.

He was on top of Horn. Now he reached along the deck for his gun which he had dropped in the fall down the companionway. Horn wrenched around, making his own grab for the gun. He missed, saw Wade's fingers close over the weapon.

The gun swivelled around. The barrel came toward Horn. He heaved himself upward. His left hand clamped on Wade's wrist. Wade's free hand pummelled his face. Again and again that fist found its mark. Darkness bobbed in front of Horn's eyes. A deadly paralysis was creeping along his muscles. Wade was shoving the gun toward him again.

Time was running out. Horn understood that thoroughly. Wade's body on top of him was a suffocating weight. The gun barrel swung dangerously near. Wade's fingers began to tighten on the stock. Wade's brutal grin grew wider and wider.

Horn marshalled his waning strength for one last effort. He exploded his whole body upward against Wade, throwing his weight into his left hand. He twisted savagely and Wade rolled half over. The gun jammed against Wade. The convulsive pressure of his own finger on the trigger drove a bullet into his heart.

For a brief instant Wade's eyes were wide open and filled with shocked amazement. Then they fluttered shut and all life drained out of him.

Horn picked himself up with a great effort. He took three reeling steps through accumulating darkness and fell flat on his face . . .

There was a rocking sensation of motion beneath Horn. It was a rhythmic movement, slow, and steady. But the darkness remained. Then, gradually, streaks of light slipped through until his eyes opened.

It was a moment before he realized that he was in his own cabin on the *Western Star.* It took another moment before he realized that some-one had hold of his hand—the left hand—and that the someone was Kay Graham.

"You took your time about waking up," she murmured. Her eyes were warm and blue and filled with relief.

Horn glanced at Kay's face, at the distinct swelling on her jaw.

"Did he hurt you?" he asked.

"It's all right now," she said. "The main thing is that it's all over."

Horn looked past her and saw Dave London and Lieutenant Haggard standing near the door. They came up to his bunk.

"It wasn't much of a fight, after all," said London.

"Any prisoners?" Horn asked.

"Half a dozen," Haggard chimed in. "Two or three of them jumped into the Missouri and got away. But, in any event, it's the end of the Jayhawkers on the Big Muddy."

"How do you feel?" Kay asked Horn anxiously.

"Fair enough," he said, and managed a grin.

"Lucky that bullet went right through your side without nicking any ribs," said Haggard. "Ferriss taped you up—says you'll be up in a day or two. Meanwhile, we're heading back to Fort Union. Things are all wound up as far as the cavalry are concerned."

"Never saw better scrappers than the U.S. cavalry."

Haggard grinned and said, "You Missouri River men do all right."

The lieutenant waited, saw that Horn was looking at Kay, and hadn't even heard his reply. Accordingly he turned to London and said with a chuckle:

"I reckon we're no longer needed here, Dave. Let's drift."

London nodded wisely and followed Haggard out of the cabin. And behind them they left an abrupt, strained silence. It was Kay who finally broke it with a question.

"Well, Bill, don't you have anything to say?"

There was a half-amused light in her eyes and Horn felt himself colouring under her intent glance.

"I was thinking of the future," he said.

"And what about the future?" she prodded.

"I was wondering where we go from here."

"Back to Fort Union," she said. "And after that perhaps another job supplying another Union army somewhere. There's still the war. Or did you forget?"

"No, I didn't forget. But I was thinking about us. We both like the river. It's been our life a long time. And for me it's always been enough until now."

"Until now?" Kay repeated, a faster breathing stirring the soft lines of her breasts.

Horn's throat grew dry and the redness stayed in his cheeks. "Damn it, Kay," he said gruffly. "You know what I'm trying to say. I want you and—"

Kay lifted her face to him. Her defences were down. She showed him in the way that only a woman in love can show a man that she was ready for him.

"If you want me you'd better start doing something about it," she said with a laugh.

"I will but I'll need some help," Horn reminded her. "I can't sit up and I've got only one good arm."

"One arm will be enough for now," Kay said and proceeded to help him in the best way she knew.

About the Author

Charles N. Heckelmann was born in New York City. He graduated from the University of Notre Dame in 1934 and for a time he was a sports writer for the *Brooklyn Daily Eagle*. He also wrote Western fiction for the pulp magazine market, beginning with "The Desert Devil" published in *Western Trails* (8/37). He contributed heavily to Standard Magazines publications and became an editor at the company, while continuing to write Western fiction himself. In 1941 he was made editor at the company's paperback publishing arm, Popular Library. His first Western novel was *Vengeance Trail* (Arcadia House, 1944). He continued publishing Western novels over the years, including among the best of these *Fighting Ramrod* (1951) and *Hell In His Holsters* (1952) for Doubleday and *The Rawhider* (1952) for Holt. Frequently his novels also ran in various of the Western magazines published by Standard Magazines prior to book publication. For example, "Fighting Ramrod" appeared in *West* (5/51) and "Hell in His Holsters" ran in *Popular Western* (12/51). For him the book of which he was especially proud was *Trumpets In The Dawn*

(1958), a major historical novel about the Custer battle at Little Big Horn. Heckelmann himself commented: "Always Westerns have been my first love. I've traveled a great deal in the West, have an extensive library of research volumes and always strive to make my books as authentic as possible. My basic idea is to provide good reading entertainment."

Center Point Large Print
600 Brooks Road / PO Box 1
Thorndike ME 04986-0001 USA

(207) 568-3717

US & Canada:
1 800 929-9108
www.centerpointlargeprint.com